THIS BOOK
~~BELONGS TO:~~
acquired by:

_____

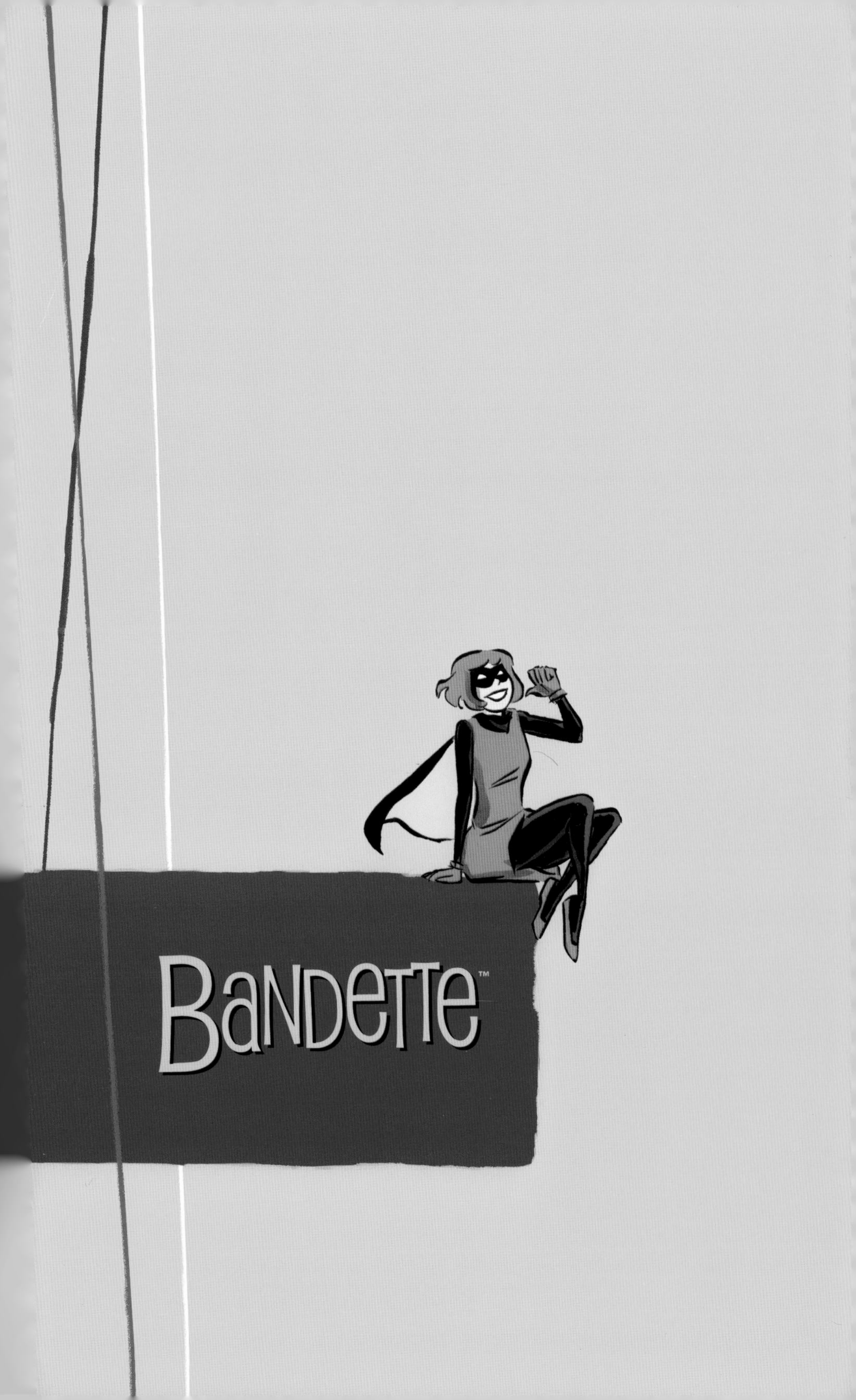
Bandette™

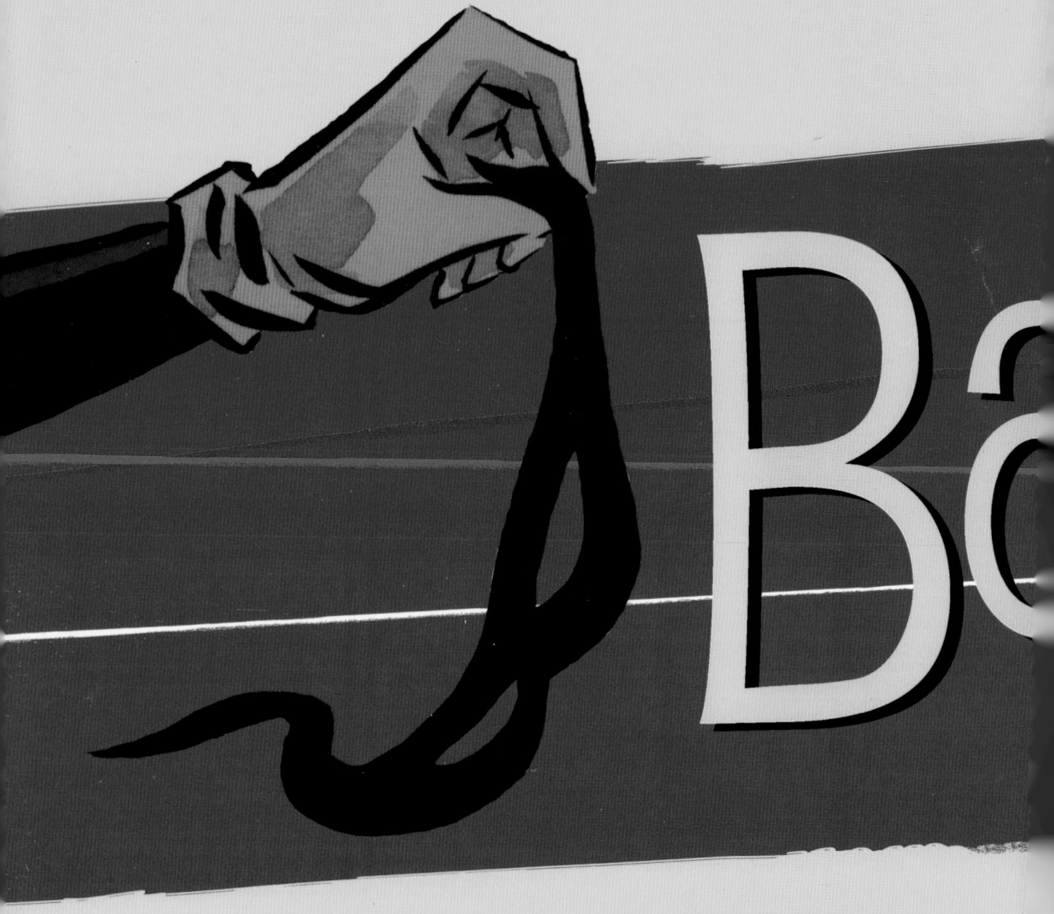
Ba

NDETTE™

in Presto!

Story by PAUL TOBIN

Art by COLLEEN COOVER

Foreword by PAUL CORNELL

DARK HORSE BOOKS

Digital Production RYAN JORGENSEN

Design IRINA BEFFA

Editor BRENDAN WRIGHT

President and Publisher MIKE RICHARDSON

BANDETTE™ VOLUME ONE: PRESTO!
© 2012, 2013 Paul Tobin and Colleen Coover. All rights reserved. Bandette and all characters prominently featured herein ar trademarks of Paul Tobin and Colleen Coover. All other material, unless otherwise specified, © 2013 Dark Horse Comics, Inc. All rights reserved. No portion of this publication may be reproduced or transmitted, in any form or by any means, without the express written permission of Dark Horse Comics, Inc., except for purposes of review. Names, characters, places, and inciden featured in this publication either are the product of the authors' imaginations or are used fictitiously. Any resemblance to actu persons (living or dead), events, institutions, or locales, without satiric intent, is coincidental. Dark Horse Books, Dark Horse Comics, and the Dark Horse logo are registered trademarks of Dark Horse Comics, Inc.

This volume collects issues one through five of the Monkeybrain comic book series *Bandette*.

Published by Dark Horse Books
A division of Dark Horse Comics, Inc.
10956 SE Main Street
Milwaukie, Oregon 97222

DarkHorse.com

Library of Congress Cataloging-in-Publication Data

Tobin, Paul, 1965- author.
 Bandette : Presto! / story by Paul Tobin ; art by Colleen Coover ; foreword by Paul Cornell. – First edition.
    pages cm
 ISBN 978-1-61655-279-4
1. Teenage girls–Comic books, strips, etc. 2. Burglars–Comic books, strips, etc. 3. Paris (France)–Comic books, strips, etc.
Graphic novels. I. Coover, Colleen, illustrator. II. Title.
 PN6727.T6B36 2013
 741.5'973–dc23
                              2013024226

First edition: November 2013

10 9 8 7 6 5 4 3 2 1
Printed in China

NEIL HANKERSON Executive Vice President • TOM WEDDLE Chief Financial Officer • RANDY STRADLEY Vice President of Publish
• MICHAEL MARTENS Vice President of Book Trade Sales • ANITA NELSON Vice President of Business Affairs • SCOTT ALLIE
Editor in Chief • MATT PARKINSON Vice President of Marketing • DAVID SCROGGY Vice President of Product Development • DAI
LAFOUNTAIN Vice President of Information Technology • DARLENE VOGEL Senior Director of Print, Design, and Production • KEN
General Counsel • DAVEY ESTRADA Editorial Director • CHRIS WARNER Senior Books Editor • DIANA SCHUTZ Executive Editor •
CARY GRAZZINI Director of Print and Development • LIA RIBACCHI Art Director • CARA NIECE Director of Scheduling • TIM WIE
Director of International Licensing • MARK BERNARDI Director of Digital Publishing

Foreword

Carefree isn't a word you could use to describe most comics these days. In a worryingly chaotic market, many comickers opt to underline the sheer dramatic seriousness and importance of every single frame, urging you to believe that this time everything will change, and that change will be terribly meaningful.

Bandette doesn't care.

She barely entertains the possibility that she might be arrested or be facing genuine danger. She has the ability to take a moment to congratulate an assassin who's trying to kill her on the cut of her cape. Which actually begins a conversation about cape shops as the fight continues.

Because she's free.

Is there a more attractive quality than *joie de vivre*, that sense that a lead character has escaped consequences, or, more accurately, is defying the mere possibility of them? Bandette declares "Presto!" as if it's a philosophy, and from her, it is. She says, "I've always wanted to say that!" and "Seriously, I'm really good at this stuff" and "A shot has rung out" as if she's grabbing hold of fictionality, deliberately living life like it's a book. (I'd say a comic, but comics haven't often been like this. And Bandette likes books.) She's up against an organization that has titles for its plans that she's supposed to recognize, as if they're novels she's been featured in. I'm a little worried that Monsieur takes these threats more seriously, because that might mean that in future issues Bandette may be threatened by the incursion of reality, but then I guess we'd just get to enjoy seeing her escape it.

One can see the influence of Francophone comics on Colleen Coover's art. Belgique shouts like Captain Haddock or Vitalstatistix. (And his initials, B. D., suggest his full name might be Bande Dessinée Belgique, *BD* being the popular phrase for comics over there. This character *is* Belgian comics!) But it's all only in suggestion; it's not like Colleen's taken on the style of one particular artist. And the world she draws is very much a modern pastiche, so the moves of a *roman policier* take place in diverse, multicultural settings. I adore how much of the story is told in body language. Look at Bandette saying, "You are old and frail, and I would not have you hurt in this clash" to Monsieur. Similarly, Paul Tobin is also having fun with the suggestion of Frenchness, putting over accents in English dialogue without resorting to phonetic spelling. Phrases like "your attention please" sound like they've been translated from a French original.

I think a 15+ age rating for *Bandette* is being rather overcareful. I'd want a daughter of mine to be reading this title from a young age, making a mask of her own and yelling "Presto!" Our heroine's strength lies not just in her willingness to ignore the values of the culture around her (fictionally and in terms of the comics market) and be her own person, but also in creating a community of friends to support her. (Hmm, I suppose she is a thief, but she steals only from those that deserve it, and mostly in order that she can read more.) I'd very much like her to read a comic that tells her she can be carefree. And free.

I'm in love with this comic, honestly, and I commend those who created it, and Chris and Allison of Monkeybrain Comics for publishing it. I have only one question. I'm still wondering how Pimento contributed to Operation Bandette. Is that him in the background, sitting on a gravestone? But to push a point like that is to be dully literal, and to go against the spirit of *presto*!

Paul Cornell
Buckinghamshire, June 2013

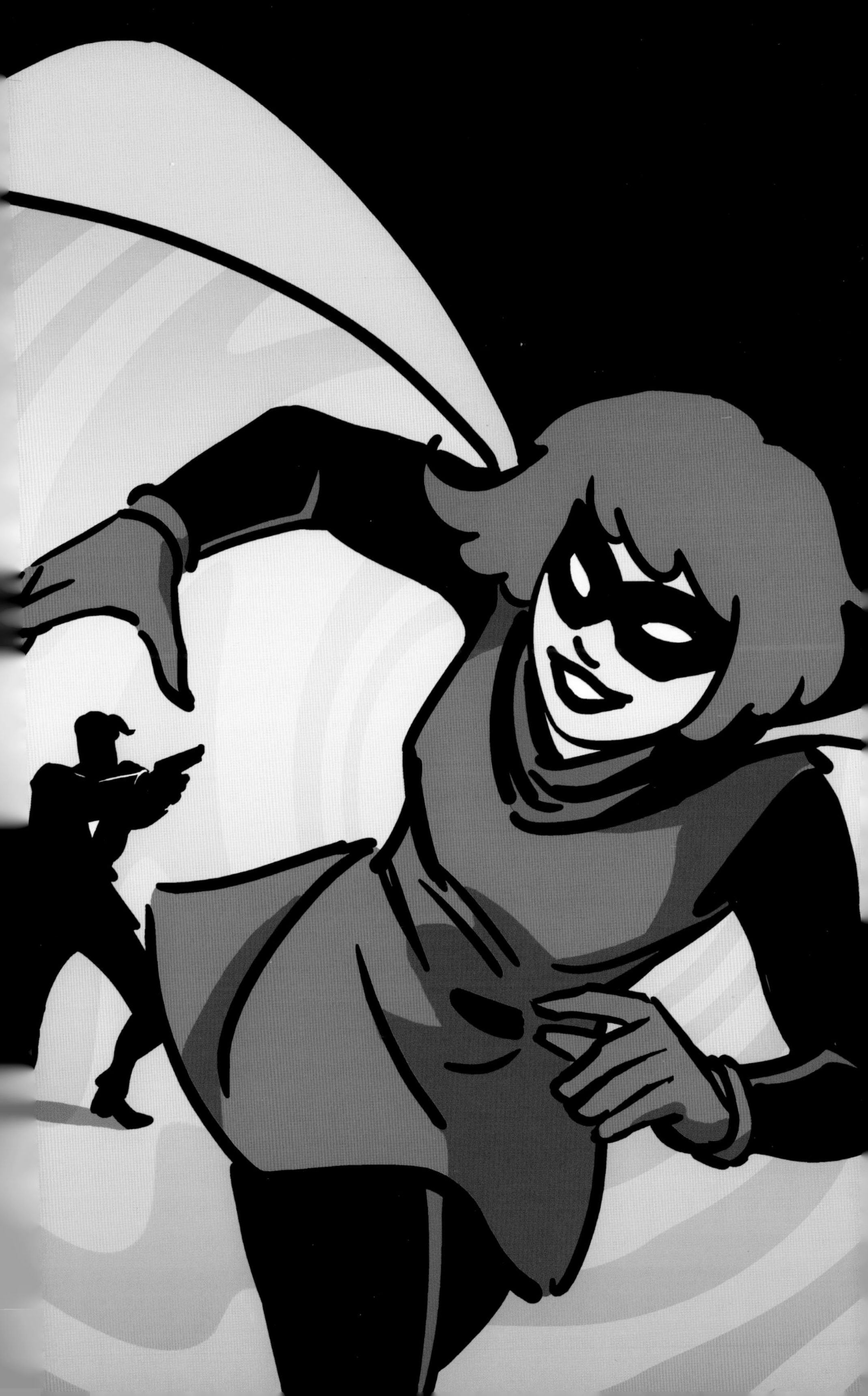

chapter one
INTRODUCING BANDETTE!

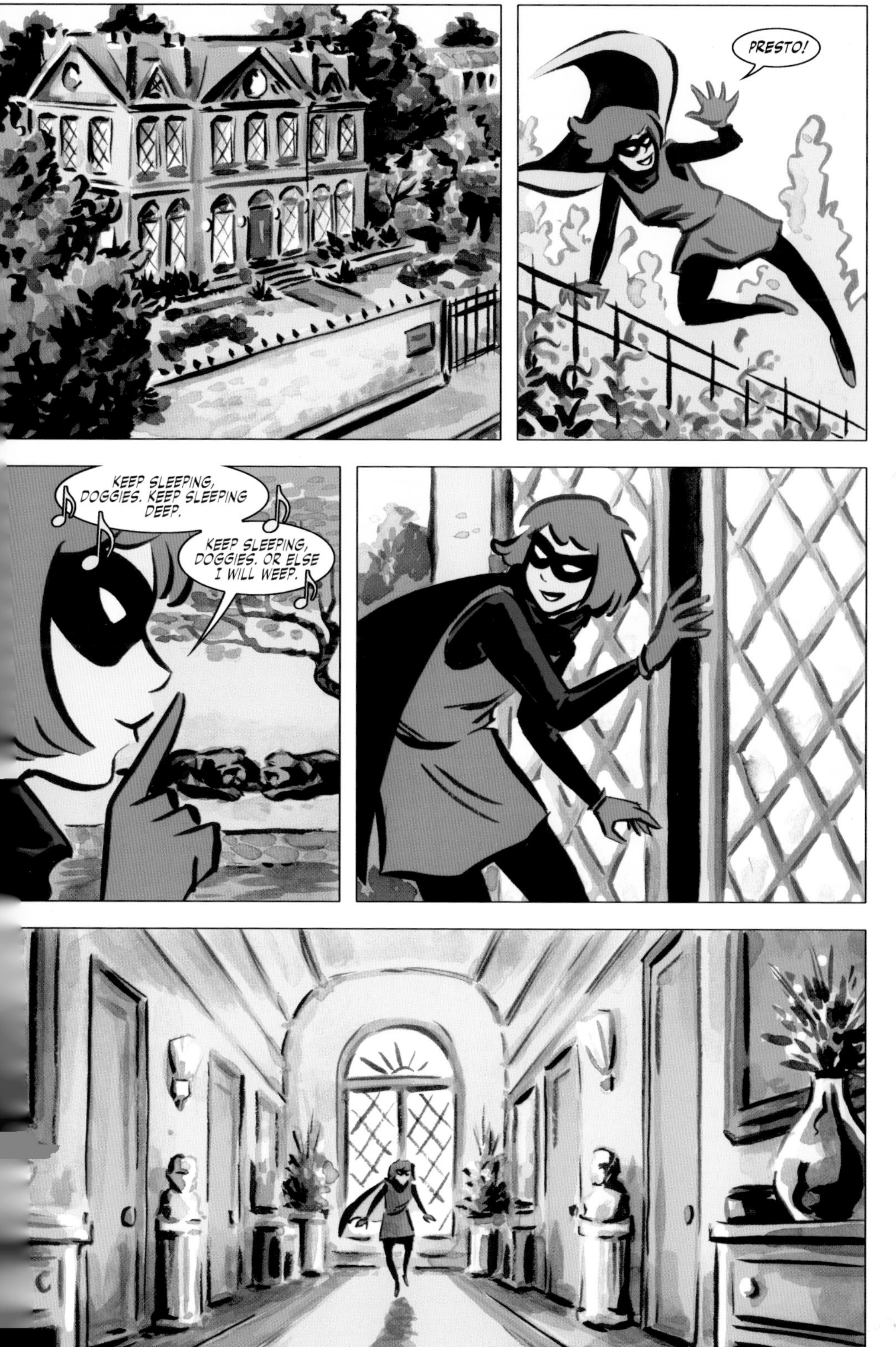
PRESTO!
KEEP SLEEPING, DOGGIES. KEEP SLEEPING DEEP.
KEEP SLEEPING, DOGGIES. OR ELSE I WILL WEEP.

OOH! ANOTHER DOGGIE.

RUFF!

HELLO, CUTIE. MY NAME IS *BANDETTE*. WANT TO COME ALONG WITH ME ON A *ROBBERY*?

REALLY? YOU *DO*?

OH, *NAUGHTY DOG!* YOU'RE AS BAD AS A *CAT!*

YOUR MASTER HAS SEVERAL DRAWINGS BY *REMBRANDT*. VERY TINY. BUT...*WOW.* THE *LINE WORK!* THE *EXPRESSIONS!*

YOU *DO* LIK[E] REMBRAND[T] DON'T YOU[?]

RUFF!

AND HOW ABOUT YOUR MASTER? YOU LIKE HIM?

HE'S KIND OF A BAD GUY, YOU KNOW. HE SELLS WEAPONS TO SOME VERY SHADY MEN, UNDER-WORLD ORGANIZATIONS, AND NASTY GOVERNMENTS.

HE'S A VERY *BUSY* BAD MAN.

AND SO...HE IS *THIEVED.*

THIS IS CALLED JUSTICE. OR *LARCE[NY]* ONE OF THE TWO[...]

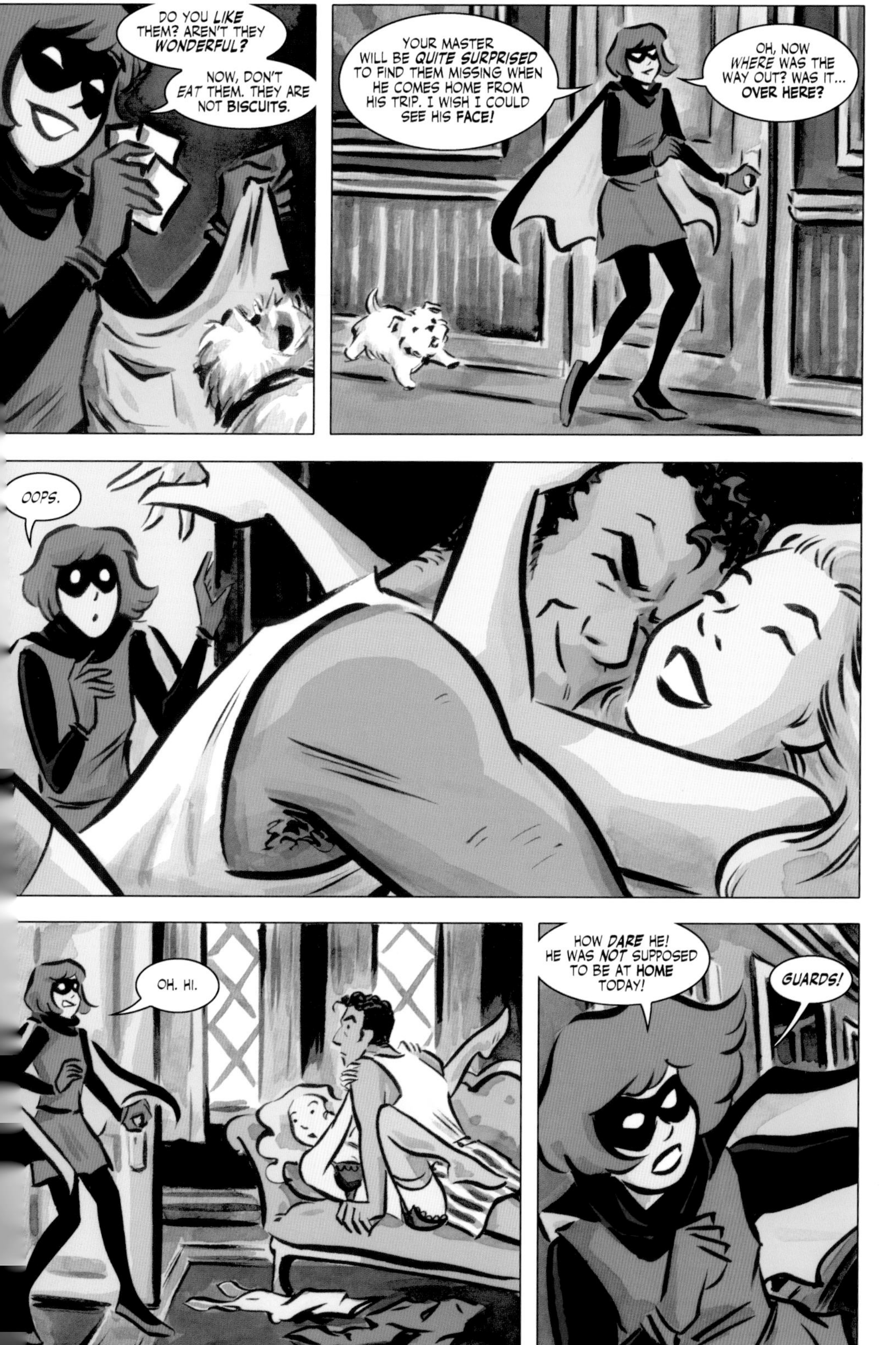
DO YOU LIKE THEM? AREN'T THEY WONDERFUL?
NOW, DON'T EAT THEM. THEY ARE NOT BISCUITS.
YOUR MASTER WILL BE QUITE SURPRISED TO FIND THEM MISSING WHEN HE COMES HOME FROM HIS TRIP. I WISH I COULD SEE HIS FACE!
OH, NOW WHERE WAS THE WAY OUT? WAS IT... OVER HERE?
OOPS.
OH. HI.
HOW DARE HE! HE WAS NOT SUPPOSED TO BE AT HOME TODAY!
GUARDS!

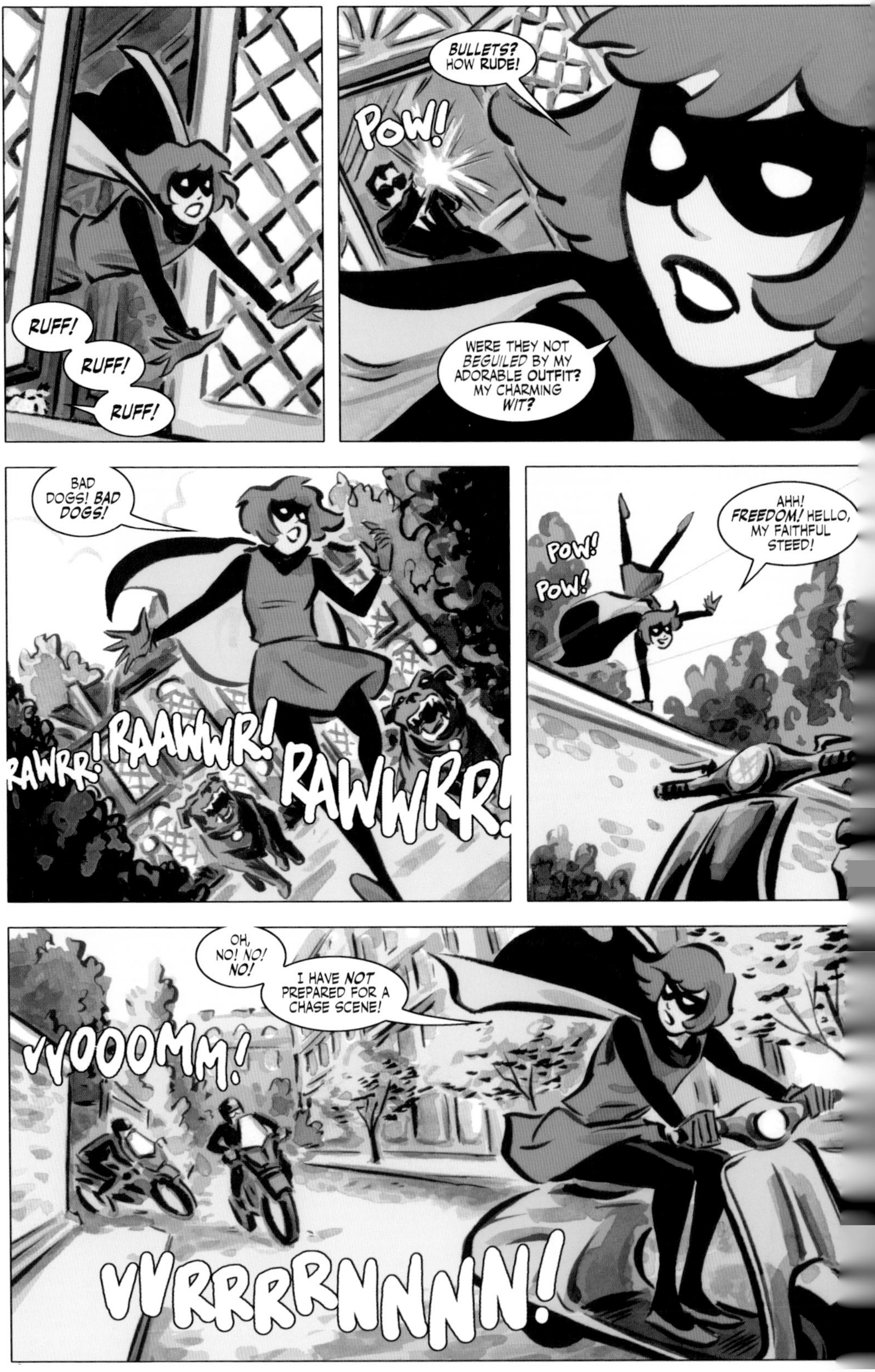
RUFF!
RUFF!
RUFF!
BULLETS? HOW RUDE!
POW!
WERE THEY NOT BEGUILED BY MY ADORABLE OUTFIT? MY CHARMING WIT?
BAD DOGS! BAD DOGS!
RAWRR! RAAWWR! RAWWRR!
POW!
POW!
AHH! FREEDOM! HELLO, MY FAITHFUL STEED!
OH, NO! NO! NO!
I HAVE NOT PREPARED FOR A CHASE SCENE!
VVOOOMM!
VVRRRRNNNN!

ELSEWHERE.

RINGG RINGG RINGG RINGG RINGG

AD THAI
KE AWAY - DEL...

'ALLO, CORVID'S RARE BOOKS AND COINS.

I NEED TO SPEAK TO MONSIEUR.

I'M AFRAID I DON'T KNOW THAT PERSON.

I BELIEVE THAT YOU DO. MY RESEARCH IS QUITE EXTENSIVE.

ALAS, MADAME, IT HAS FAILED YOU IN THIS INSTANCE. I CANNOT HELP YOU. C'EST LA VIE, LIFE WILL GO ON.

OF COURSE IT WILL.

AND I WILL FIND SOMEONE ELSE TO STEAL THE 1794 AMERICAN FLOWING HAIR DOLLAR COIN.

DID YOU SAY THE FLOWING HAIR DOLLAR? 1794?

I DID. AND I HAPPEN TO KNOW THE SAME COLLECTION HOLDS A FIRST EDITION OF THE SCARECROW OF OZ, WHICH WOULD BE PART OF MONSIEUR'S PAYMENT FOR THIS PILFERING.

AN INTERESTING BOOK, BUT HARDLY ENOUGH TO DRAW IN SOMEONE LIKE MONSIEUR.

13

PERHAPS NOT. BUT WHAT IF I WERE TO ADD THAT IT WAS ORIGINALLY THE POSSESSION OF *H.P. LOVECRAFT*, AND THAT HE MADE EXTENSIVE NOTES FOR HIS *CTHULHU MYTHOS* IN ITS MARGINS?

BONJOUR, MR. CORVID!

I HAVE YOUR LUNCH ORDER!

PAD THAI AND JASMINE TEA.

PERFECT TIMING. I'M FAMISHED.

KEEP THE *CHANGE*, DANIEL.

THANK YOU, M CORVID VERY KI OF YO

THIS IS *MONSIEUR*.

I AM INTERESTED.

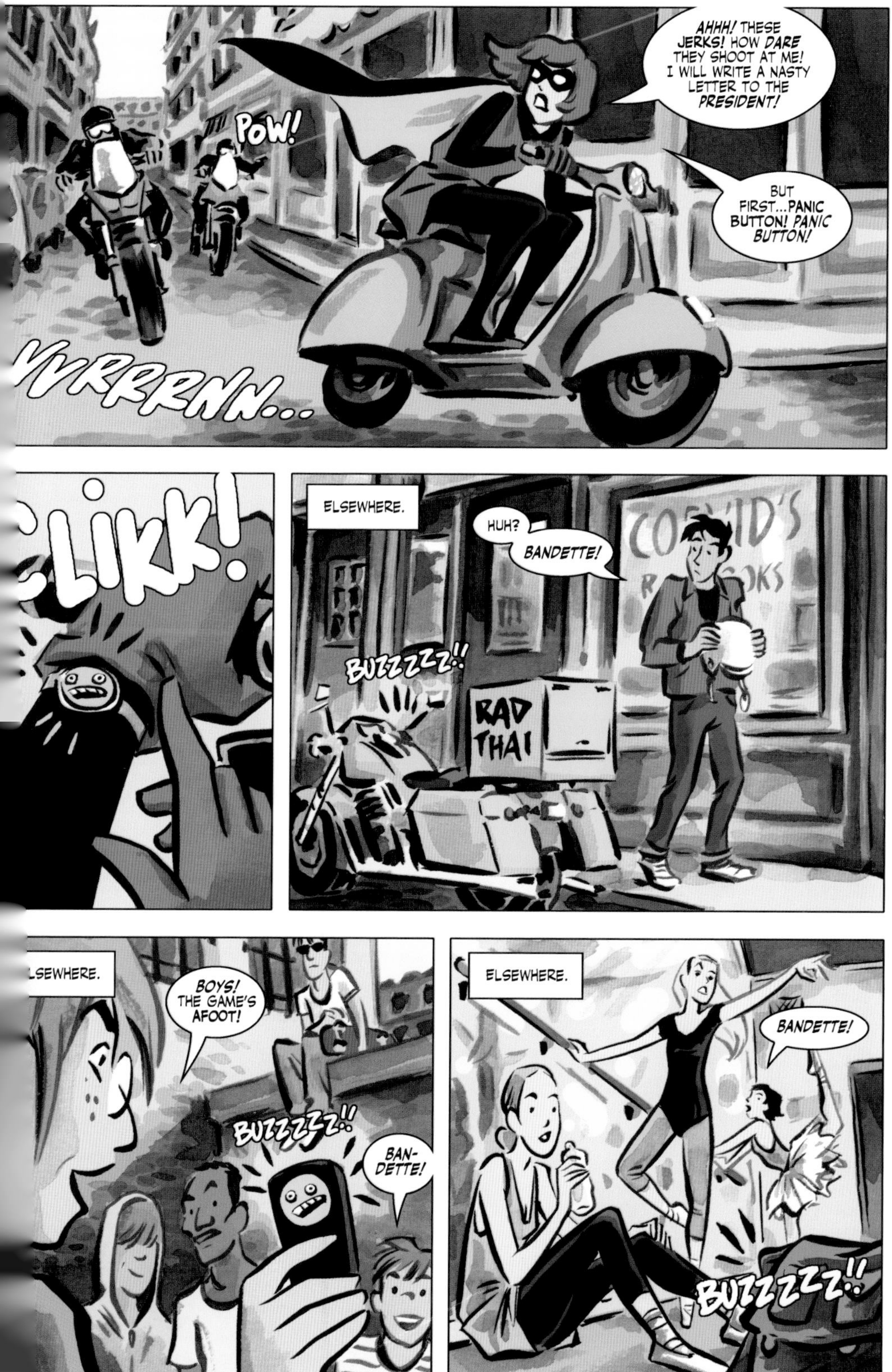

AHHH! THESE JERKS! HOW DARE THEY SHOOT AT ME! I WILL WRITE A NASTY LETTER TO THE PRESIDENT!
POW!
BUT FIRST...PANIC BUTTON! PANIC BUTTON!
VVRRRNN...
CLIKK!
ELSEWHERE.
HUH?
BANDETTE!
BUZZZZZ!!
RAD THAI
LSEWHERE.
BOYS! THE GAME'S AFOOT!
BUZZZZZ!!
BAN-DETTE!
ELSEWHERE.
BANDETTE!
BUZZZZZ!!

ELSEWHERE.

INSPECTOR *BELGIQUE!*

WHAT'S THE SITUATION?

BANK ROBBERY GONE POORLY. FIVE HOSTAGES, I'M AFRAID.

DO WE HAVE A PHONE LINE?

THEY **REFUSE** TO ANSWER.

SNIPERS HAVE A SHOT?

NO. THE ANGLES ARE BAD.

WHAT ABOUT GAS, THEN CHARGING IN THROUGH THE FRONT?

TOO MUCH RISK TO THE HOSTAGES.

AHHH. WHAT DO WE DO? WHAT DO WE *DO?*

MAYBE... MAYBE YOU SHOULD MAKE THE CALL?

GRUMBLE GRUMBLE

JUST *ONCE*, I'D LIKE TO BE ABLE TO DO IT ON MY OWN. MAKE AN ARREST ALL BY *MYSELF*.

THE THOUGHT OF CALLING FOR HELP MAKES MY *UNDERWEAR* RIDE UP THE CRACK OF MY *ASS*.

I DON'T LIKE IT ALL THAT MUCH *MYSELF*. THE *CALL*, I MEAN. I'M TRYING *NOT* TO THINK ABOUT YOUR UNDERWEAR.

BUT THE *TRUTH* IS THAT WE ARE ALL IN THIS FIGHT *TOGETHER*, BELGIQUE. WHETHER OR NOT YOU MAKE THAT CALL, *NONE* OF US CAN DO THIS *ALONE*.

YOU'RE RIGHT. THIS IS NO TIME TO PLAY *LONE WOLF*. THERE ARE LIVES AT STAKE.

AHH. DAMN THIS *DAY*. AND DAMN THIS *UNDERWEAR*.

BEEP DEEP B-DEEP

17

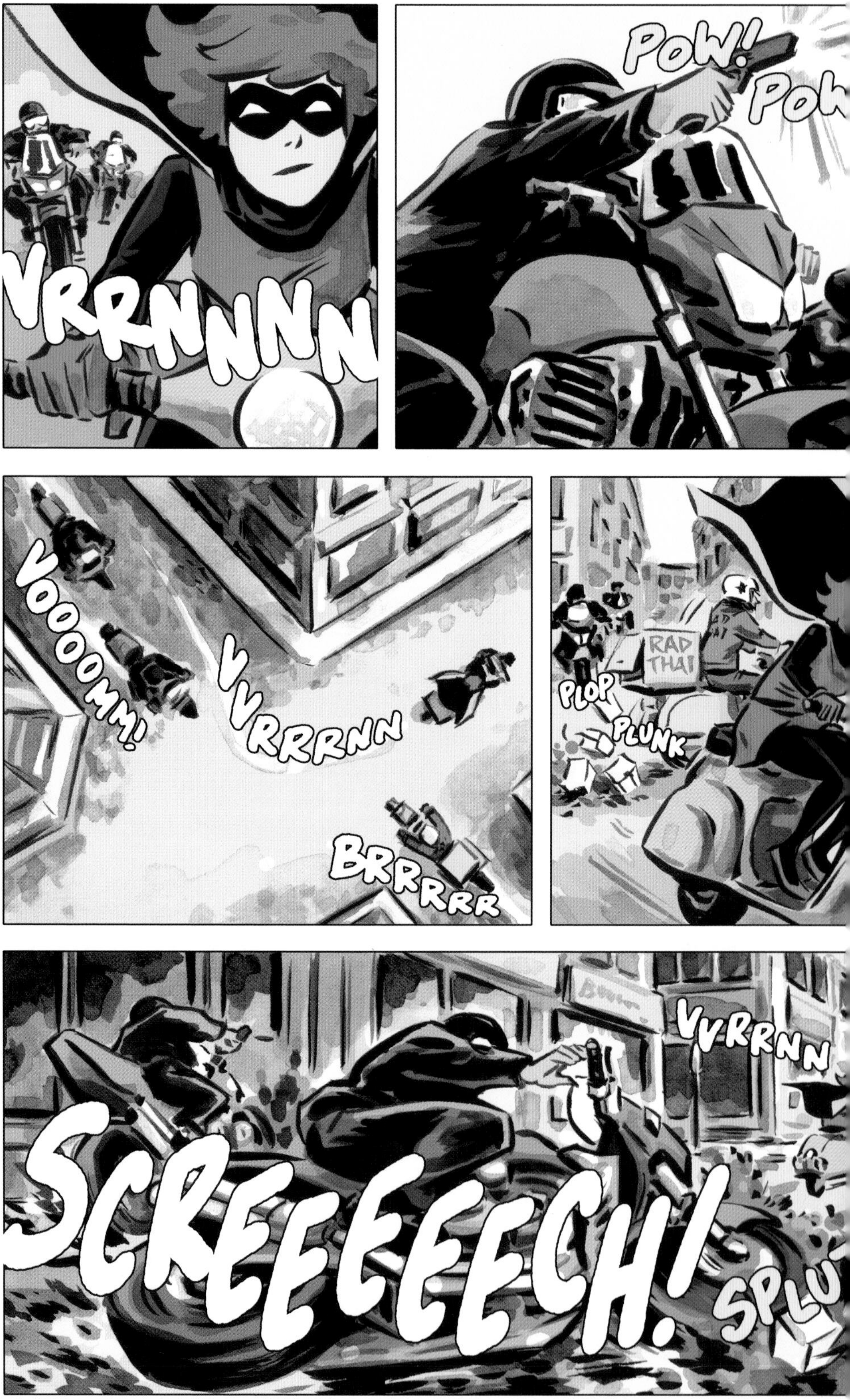
VRRNNNNN
POW!
POW
VOOOOMM!
VVRRRNN
BRRRRRR
RAD THAI
PLOP
PLUNK
VVRRNNN
SCREEEEEECH!
SPLU

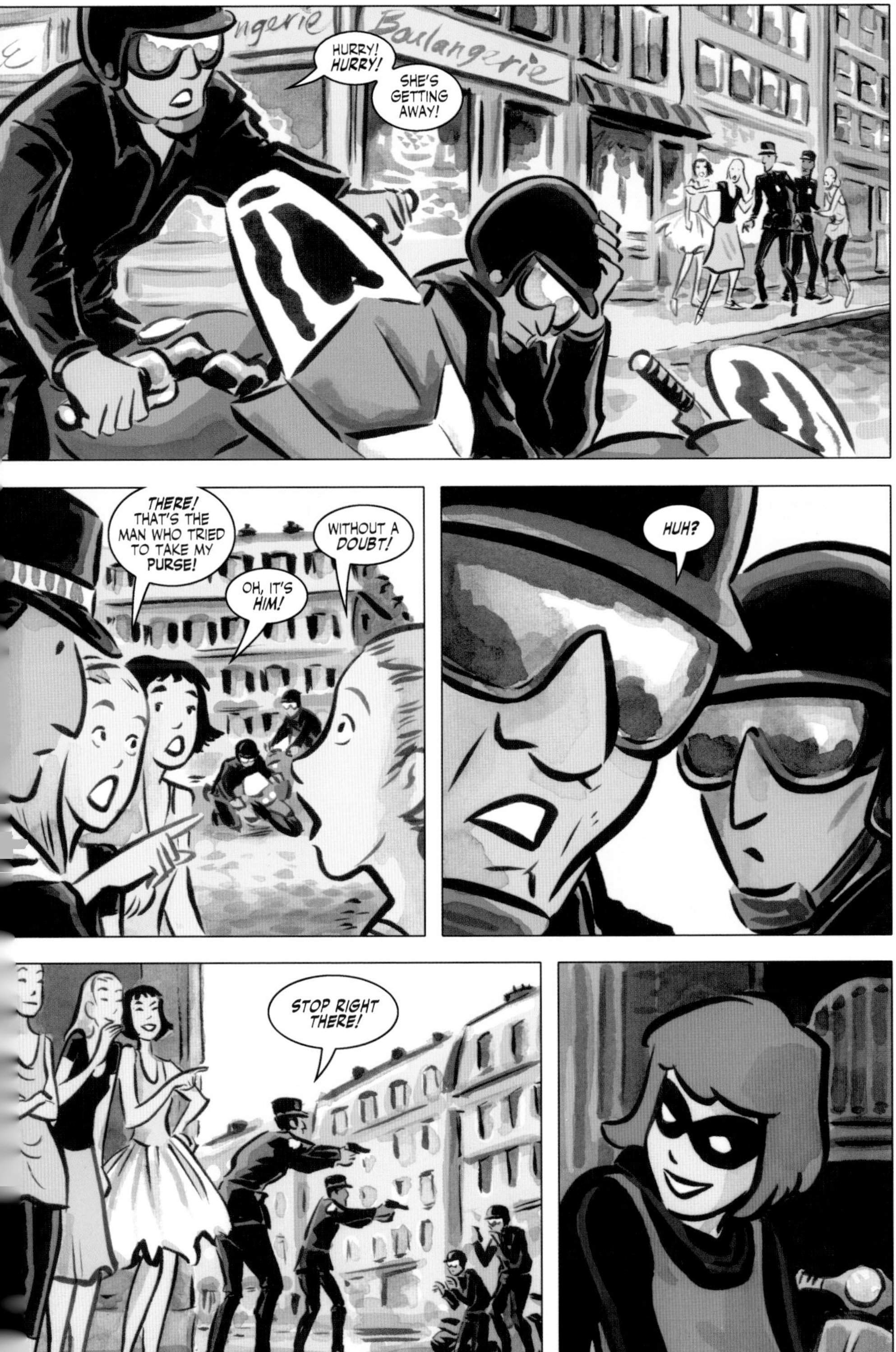
Boulangerie
HURRY! HURRY!
SHE'S GETTING AWAY!
THERE! THAT'S THE MAN WHO TRIED TO TAKE MY PURSE!
OH, IT'S HIM!
WITHOUT A DOUBT!
HUH?
STOP RIGHT THERE!

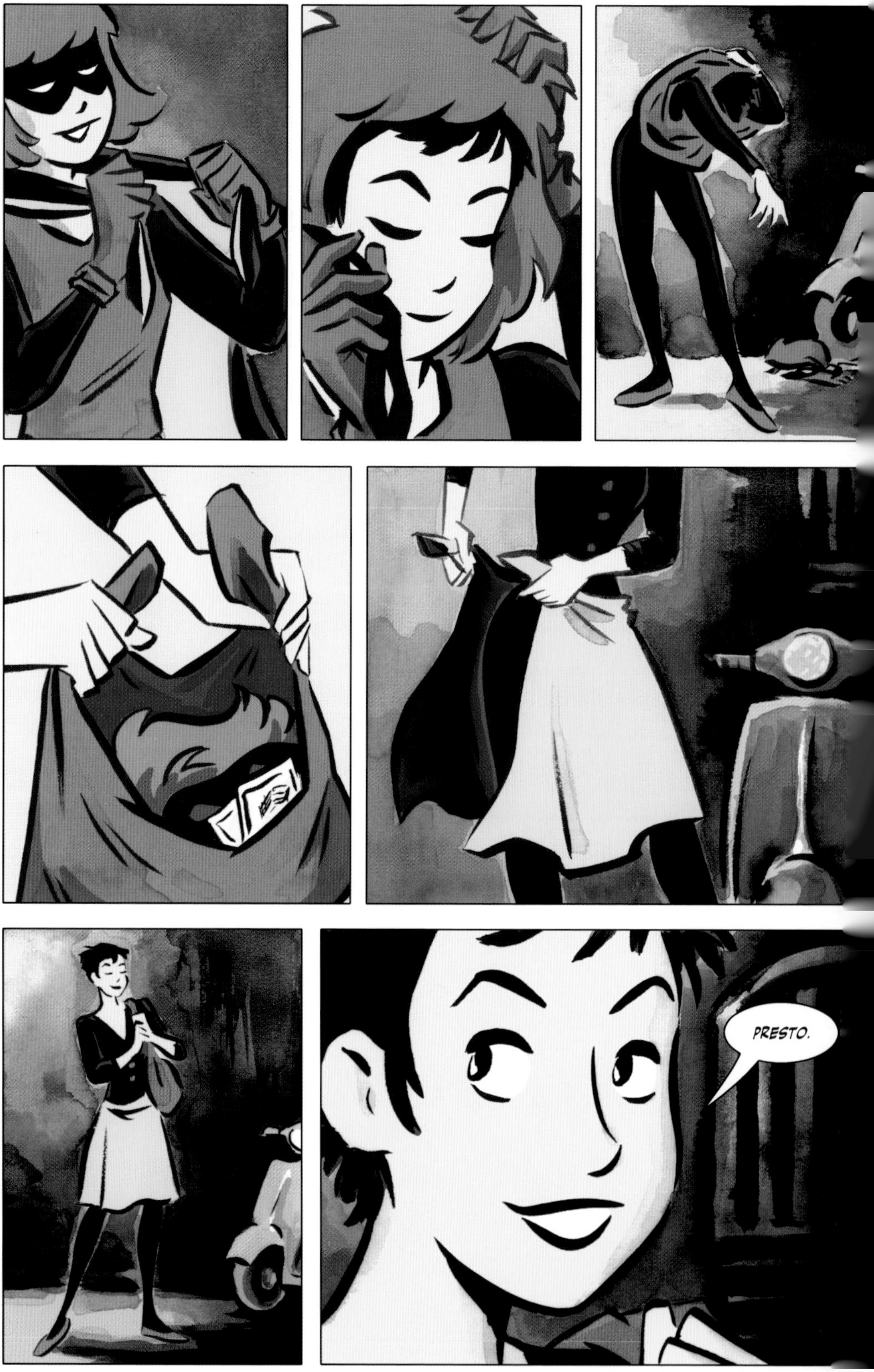
PRESTO.

OH? MY PHONE?

BUZZZ
♪RING! RING!♪
BUZZZ

'ALLO?

BANDETTE. IT'S ME.

BANQU

INSPECTOR BELGIQUE.

POLICE

I NEED YOUR HELP.

21

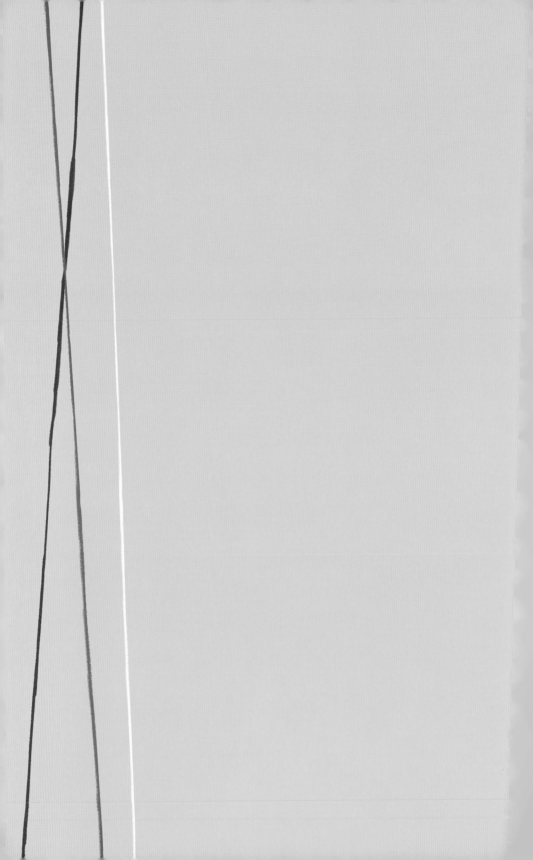

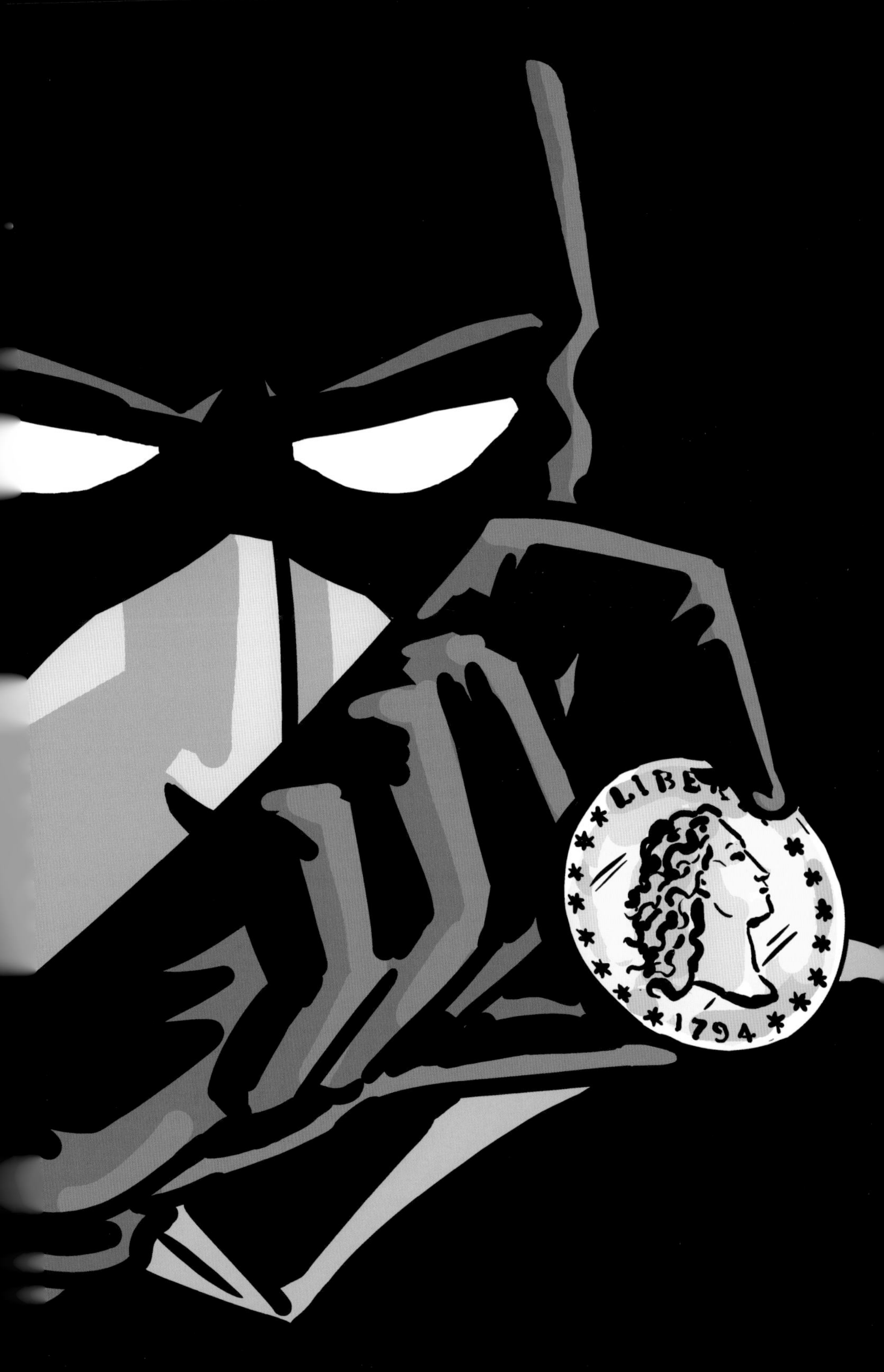
1794

chapter two
KNOCKOUT!

DIDN'T BANDETTE SAY SHE WOULD HELP?

SHE DID.

WELL THEN...WHERE IS SHE?

"I HAVE NO IDEA."

GET THE MONEY READY! GET IT *READY!*

WE READY TO MOVE? HOW WILL WE GET PAST THE POLICE?

I'M GONNA MAKE THE CALL. THEY'LL DO WHAT WE SAY, OR WE'LL KILL ONE OF THE HOSTAGES.

OOOOH-LA-LA! LOOK AT ALL THIS *MONEY!* KIND OF MAKES ME WANT TO BE A CRIMINAL.

MORE OF A CRIMINAL, I MEAN.

WELL, A DIFFERENT *SORT* OF CRIMINAL.

TIME TO MAKE SOME CALLS, BANDETTE.

YOU HAVE MADE PROMISES, AN THEY MUST B KEPT.

READY TO PLAY SOME *BASEBALL?*

READY, BANDETTE!

BELGIQUE? IT'S BANDETTE. LET THE ROBBERS HAVE THE MONEY.

WHA-A-T!?

%&$*.

OH, YES. I UNDERSTAND. GOOD POINT.

@!%*!!

&ØÆ?!!

OH, MY! SUCH LANGUAGE!

GOOD MAN. GOOD MAN. GET IT ALL OUT. YOU KNOW BANDETTE'S MEDICINES ARE BEST IN THE END.

Π*i#&!!

TWENTYFIVE *@£!!YEARSON THEFORCE@$!!& ANOTHERHEART ATTACK%!!*# RABBITBACKIN THE#@!!& HAT!!!

AHHHH! WHY DOES SHE ALWAYS MAKE THINGS SO HARD?

WHY DO YOU NEVER BELIEVE SHE HAS A PLAN?

INSPECTOR... WHAT SHALL WE...?

POLICE

LET THEM HAVE THE MONEY.

LET THEM...

SIR...?

ET THEM HAVE THE MONEY!

LET THEM HAVE THE MONEY?

YOU'RE... LETTING US HAVE THE MONEY?

THAT'S RIGHT, YOU LOSERS...YOU JUST LET US *HAVE* THE MONEY!

VRRRRRMM...

WE'RE RICH!

NOT SURE WHY THEY SUDDENLY DECIDED TO LET US TAKE THE MONEY, BUT, HEY, IF SOMEONE LETS ME GET AWAY WITH MILLIONS...I'LL DO IT!

AND IF THEY DO TRY TO STOP US, WE STILL HAVE OUR HOSTAGES FOR INSURANCE! HA HA!

CRAKK!

HEY! GET OUT OF THE WAY!

WHAT? NO WAY!

WE'LL ONLY MOVE FOR YOU IF...

YOU DEFEAT US IN BASEBALL!

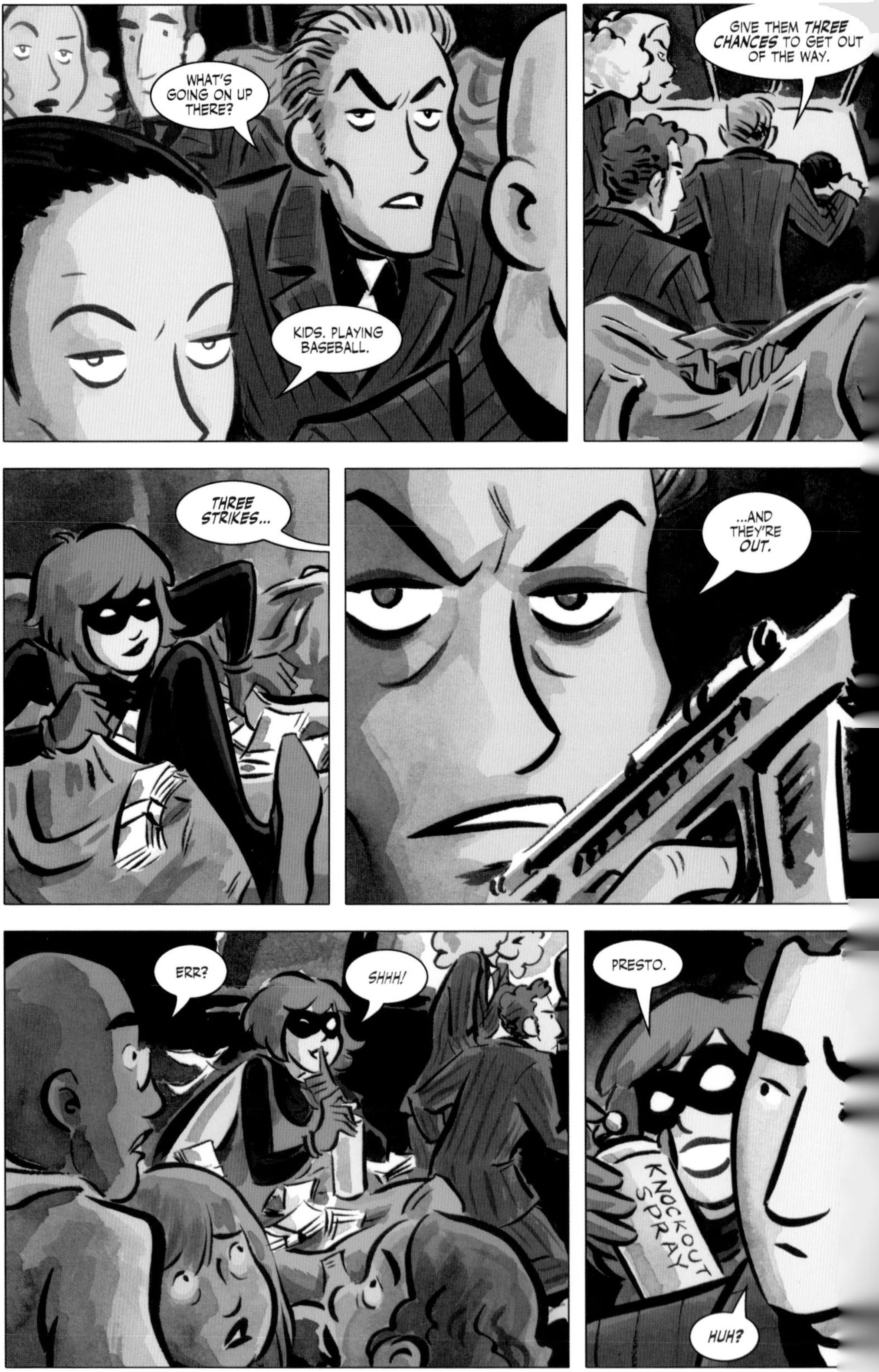
WHAT'S GOING ON UP THERE?
KIDS. PLAYING BASEBALL.
GIVE THEM THREE CHANCES TO GET OUT OF THE WAY.
THREE STRIKES...
...AND THEY'RE OUT.
ERR?
SHHH!
PRESTO.
KNOCKOUT SPRAY
HUH?

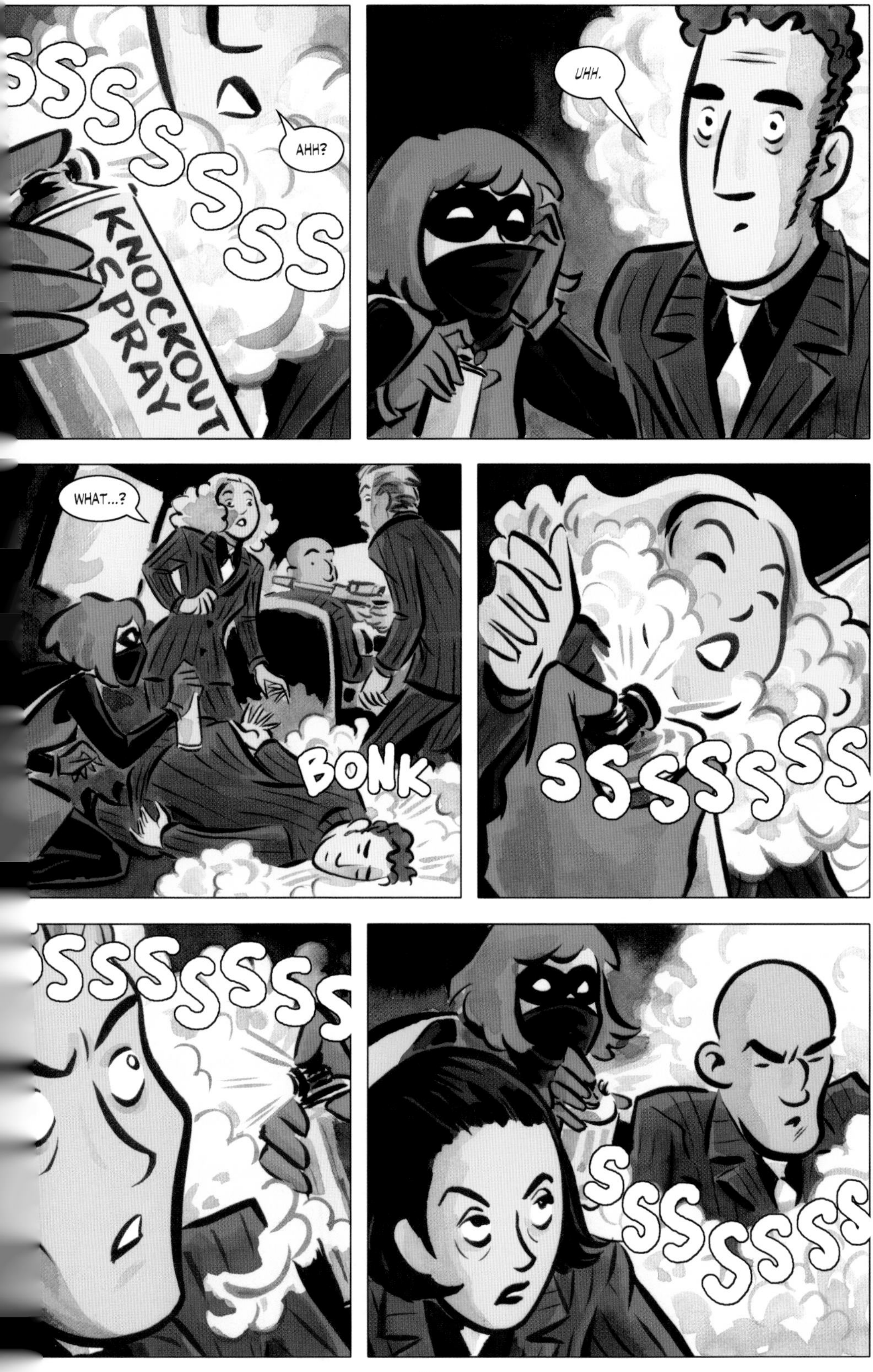
SSSSSSSSS
KNOCKOUT SPRAY
AHH?
UHH.
WHAT...?
BONK
SSSSSSS
SSSSSSS
SSSSSSSSS

AH, JUST WHO I WANTED TO SEE!

BRRR

DANIEL... DO YOU KNOW HOW TO DRIVE THIS VAN?

THIS? BUT OF COURSE!

OH, *GOOD!* I *KNEW* I COULD COUNT ON YOU!

BE A DEAR AND TAKE IT BACK TO INSPECTOR BELGIQUE AT THE BANK FOR ME, PLEASE!

EXCELL WORK, EV ONE

VRRRNNN

SPLASH!

RAWWAAAARRR!!!

OOOH! A TRAGEDY! YOU POOR THING.

HERE YOU GO, MY FRIEND.

NO NEED TO *THANK* ME, AS IT'S THE VERY *LEAST* I CAN DO. AFTER ALL...

SCRUB SCRUB

...I OWN THIS PUDDLE.

NOW THEN, I WOULD MAKE YOU VOW TO KEEP MY SECRETS, BUT *YOU* ARE A *CAT.*

CLIK!

RUMBLE!

...AND NO CAT HAS *EVER* GIVEN AWAY A SECRET.

SO ALL IS *GOOD,* NO?

BEEP
BEEP
BEEP

MY *DEAR* BELGIQUE! IT'S ME, *BANDETTE!*

HAS MY *HANDSOME* DELIVERY BOY ARRIVED?

HE'S *HERE,* YES.

AND I TRUST ALL IS *WELL?*

WELL... THE MONEY *IS* ACCOUNTED FOR AND THE HOSTAGES *ARE* UNHARMED.

TELL HER SHE DID A *GOOD* JOB.

TELL HER SHE DID A *GOOD JOB!* SHOW THAT YOUNG GIRL SOME *APPRECIATION!* YOU'RE *NEVER* NICE TO HER!

WHAT?

SHE'S A *CRIMINAL!*

WHAT'S *CRIMINAL* IS THE WAY YOU *TREAT* HER.

TELL HER SHE *DID WE* IS THAT *S* HARD?

34

ERR, BANDETTE...

YES, INSPECTOR? *YES?* YOU HAVE SOMETHING TO *SAY?*

BANDETTE. LIEUTENANT PRICE WANTS ME TO TELL YOU THAT...

MADAME PRESTO

MISTRESS of MYSTERY

AHEM. I MEAN, I WANT TO SAY...

SORRY, I HAVE TO *GO.*

YOU SHOULD GIVE DANIEL A *KISS* FOR ME!

IT'S VERY *CUTE* WHEN HE GETS *EMBARRASSED!*

GOODBYE!

CLIKK!

NOW THEN, WHO *ELSE* NEEDS A CALL?

AHHH, SO *MUCH* TO DO! SO MUCH TO DO!

AH, *PIMENTO!* ONE MOMENT! I'M MAKING A CALL!

YIP!

BANDETTE SAYS WE DID A *FANTASTIC* JOB!

HURRAH! WE ARE THE *BEST!*

YOUR *ATTENTION,* PLEASE! BANDETTE SAYS WE ARE *ANGELS!*

SUCH A *COMPLIMENT* FROM THE DEVIL *HERSELF!*

D'ORSAY ARTS INSURANCE ~ CLAIMS DIVISION

RING RING RING RING

'ALLO, CLAIMS DIVISION.

WHAT'S *THAT?* YOU'VE RECOVERED THE MISSING *REMBRANDTS? JOY!*

YOU'LL HAVE YOUR *USUAL REWARD* CHECK IN THE MAIL! THANK YOU *SO MUCH,* BANDETTE!

OH. YOU WERE ONLY ABLE TO FIND *THREE* OF THEM? WHAT A *PITY.*

I WONDER WHAT HAPPENED TO THE *FOURTH?*

YES. I WONDER AS WELL.

AHH, PERHAPS ONE DAY IT WILL *TURN UP.*

YIP!

OH, *BANDETTE,* YOU ARE A *SAUCE.*

NOW THEN, WHAT'S *NEXT?* SHALL I INFILTRATE THE *CRIMINAL UNDERWORLD?* BREAK A BOY'S HEART?

PERHAPS I SHOULD TREAT MY *URCHINS* TO BANDETTE'S VERY OWN BEST BAKED *CUPCAKES?*

OR, *HMMM,* EVEN THE *MAJESTIC* NEED TO REST.

MAYBE A *GOOD BOOK?*

FIRST EDITIONS: PURCHASED

FIRST EDITION LIBERATED

Thank you for your donation. Sincerely, Monsieur

MUMMERRUMBLE
MUMMER *BANDETTE*
RUMBLEMUMBLE

EH?

DID I
HEAR...THAT
NAME?

RUMEMBR
*BANDETTE*RUMBL
RUMBLEMM.

38

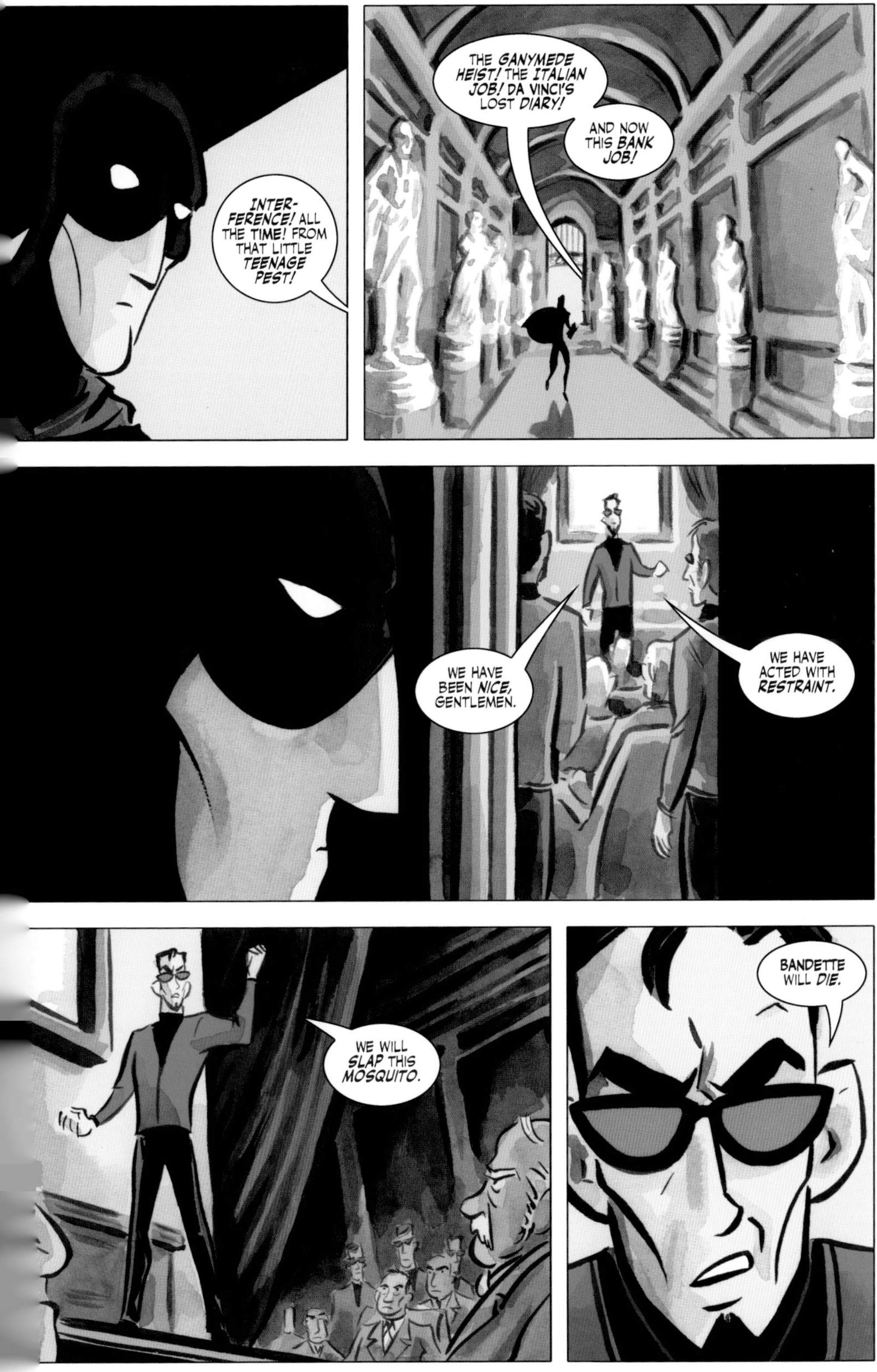
INTER-FERENCE! ALL THE TIME! FROM THAT LITTLE TEENAGE PEST!
THE GANYMEDE HEIST! THE ITALIAN JOB! DA VINCI'S LOST DIARY!
AND NOW THIS BANK JOB!
WE HAVE BEEN NICE, GENTLEMEN.
WE HAVE ACTED WITH RESTRAINT.
WE WILL SLAP THIS MOSQUITO.
BANDETTE WILL DIE.

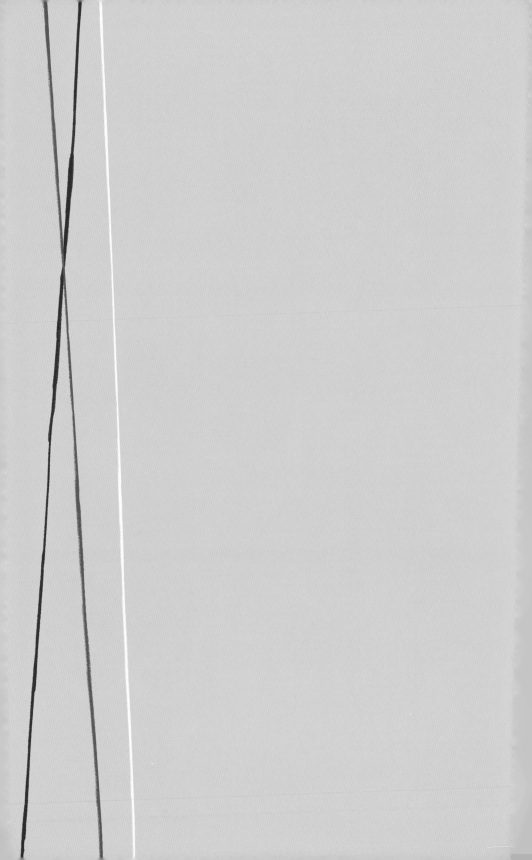

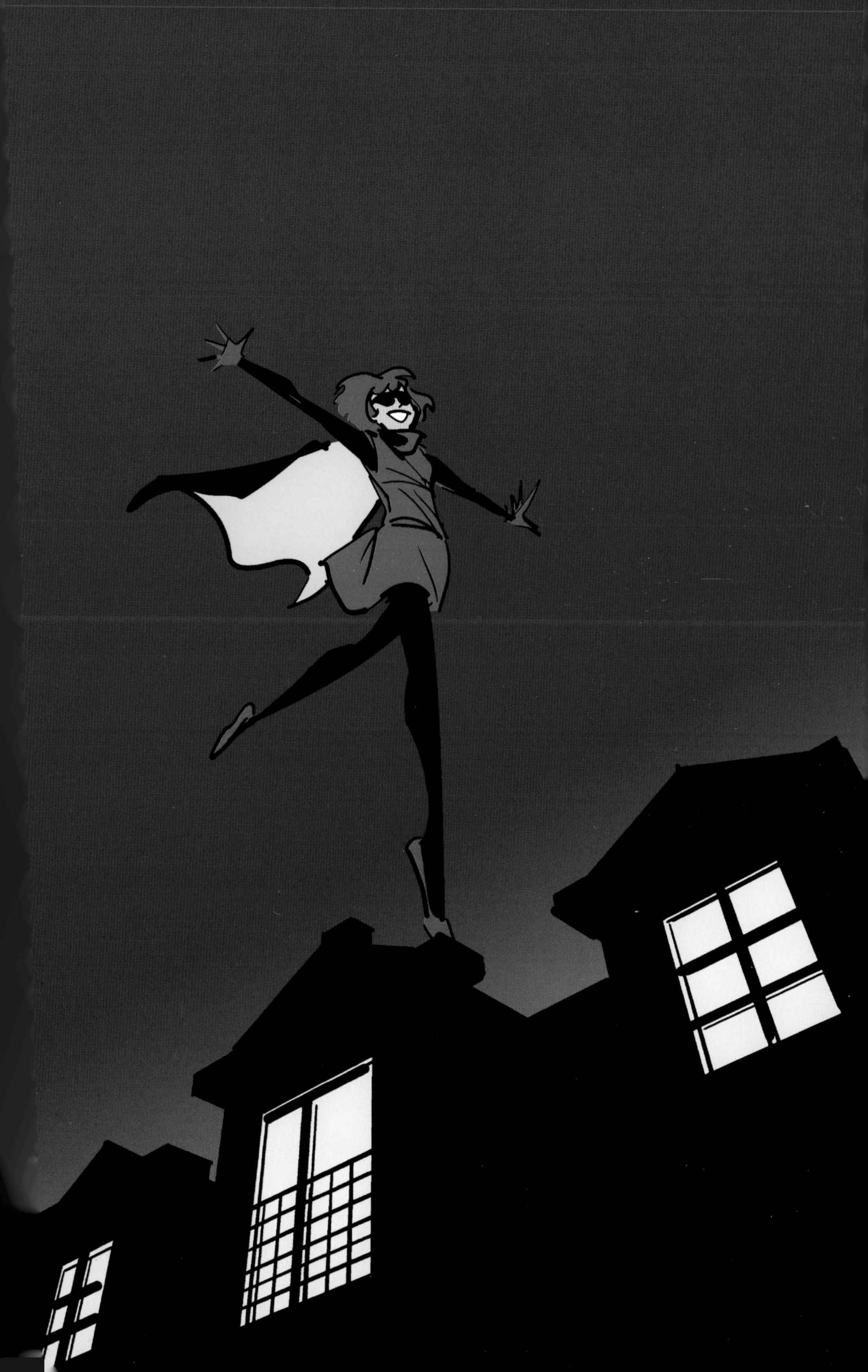

chapter three
MEETING AT MIDNIGHT!

TODAY, WE LOOK AT THE ORGANIZATION KNOWN AS THE *FRIENDS IN NEED IMPROVEMENT SOCIETY.*

OR, AS SOME PEOPLE CALL THEM: *FINIS.*

OSTENSIBLY, *FINIS* WORKS TO IMPROVE THE PLIGHT OF THE WORLD'S IMPOVERISHED. BUT *IS* THAT THEIR *TRUE* PURPOSE?

AFTER PULLING BACK THE CURTAIN, WE AT CHANNEL HRG-A HAVE DISCOVERED...

"BOMBING ATTACKS!"

BOOM!

MINISTÈRE D'ÉTAT

"VICE!

"ARMS TRADING!

DANGER

DANG

43

"POLITICAL MANIPULATION!

"AND... MURDER!"

THIS REPORTER HAS BEEN PROVIDED WITH A *WEALTH* OF DAMNING EVIDENCE CONCERNING *FINIS*--

--BROUGHT FORTH BY THE *ENIGMATIC* ROGUE KNOWN ONLY AS *BANDETTE.*

I'M MONTY LOMBARD, AND TODAY I'M ASKING YOU--

--IF IT'S NOT AN END TO HUNGER AND POVERTY THAT *FINIS* WANTS...

...THE WHAT IT?

HELLO. WHAT'S *THIS?*

BANDETTE:
WE NEED TO SPEAK.
TUESDAY AT MIDNIGHT
WHERE MALLEVILLE
KISSES JANE.
—*Monsieur*

HMMM.
THIS IS VERY
DISTRESSING.

HOW DOES *HE* KNOW OF THIS *KISS?*

BZZZZZ
BZZZZZ

DANIEL!

'ALLO?

BANDETTE!
HAVE YOU SEEN
THE POSTERS?

OUI! I'M
LOOKING AT ONE
AT THIS VERY
MOMENT!

WE'VE
BEEN FINDING
THEM ALL OVER
THE CITY. *ALL
OVER!*

HALAL KABAB

"ON ROOFTOPS!"

ANOTHER ONE, OVER HERE!

"WITH STREET MUSICIANS!"

I WENT ONE TIME, ONE TIME, WITH A TWO-TIMING GIRL!

HE SPENDS HIS *FREE TIME*, *FREE TIME*, WITH A *TWO TIMING GIRL*

"ON POLICE CARS!"

"¡@#$*%!¬"

Bistro

"THEY'RE EVERYWHERE!"

HOW STRANGE. HOW *VERY* STRANGE.

SKRITCH SKREECH

GATHER UP OUR FORCES! SUSPEND ALL UNNECESSARY OPERATIONS! CALL AN EMERGENCY MEETING! AND DANIEL...

YES?

COU YOU PR SNACK THE ME I SHOUL MUCH SOME BARS, PLE

SOON.

GRAB!

SCRABBLE!

SNATCH!

MONSIEUR!

I NEED NOT POINT OUT HOW *IRRITATING* THIS WRETCHED MAN HAS PROVEN HIMSELF TO BE!

INSTEAD, I NEED ONLY ASK MY *DANIEL*... WHO IS THE MOST **TALENTED** THIEF THIS WORLD HAS *EVER* KNOWN?

YOU ARE.

CORRECT!

BUT... WHO IS MY **GREATEST RIVAL**?

MONSIEUR.

ALSO CORRECT.

"IT WAS *MONSIEUR* WHO BEAT ME TO NAPOLEON'S CAPE OF GOLD!"

OH! *DRAT!*

"IT WAS *HE* WHO ABSCONDED WITH **THE SECRET DIARIES OF MADAME DE POMPADOUR!**"

C'EST UNE TRAGÉDIE!!! I WANTED TO *READ* THOSE!

"AND IT WAS *HE* WHO DISCOVERED, AND *STOLE*, THE THIRTY-SIXTH VERMEER!"

OH NO NO *NO!* YOU *DEVIL!*

I THINK I MUST MAKE THIS RENDEZVOUS. MY CURIOSITY IS PIQUED.

IT WAS *CURIOSITY* THAT KILLED THE CAT.

BOREDOM HAS KILLED MANY MORE CATS THAN CURIOSITY.

YIP!

HUSH, PIMENTO.

HOW WILL YOU KNOW WHERE TO *FIND* HIM?

"WHERE *MALLEVILLE KISSES JANE?*"

WHAT DOE[S] THAT EVE[N] *MEAN?*

I WILL TELL *YOU*. AND *ONLY* YOU.

IT REFERS TO MY GRANDFATHER, *MALLEVILLE*.

ALTHOUGH THEY NEVER MET, HE WAS A GRAND ADMIRER OF *JANE AVRIL*, THE BAWDY *CANCAN* DANCER.

"WHEN MY GRANDFATHER *DIED*, MY FAMILY SCATTERED HIS ASHES OVER MME AVRIL'S GRAVE IN THE CEMETERY OF *PÈRE-LACHAISE*.

"THAT *MUST* BE THE MEETING PLACE TO WHICH *MONSIEUR* IS REFERRING."

BUT *HOW* DOES *MONSIEUR* KNOW ABOUT THIS? YOU *NEVER* TALK OF YOUR FAMILY! THIS IS THE FIRST I'VE EVER...

YES, IT IS QUITE STRANGE.

VERY WORRISOME.

I *CAN'T* LET YOU GO *ALONE!*

AH! MY *VALIANT HERO!* BUT DO NOT *WORRY.* YOU WILL BE COMING ALONG.

IN FACT... YOU *ALL* WILL.

SPECIAL POLICE HEADQUARTERS.

YOU SHOULDN'T SMOKE IN THE *ELEVATOR*, SIR.

I *SHOULDN'T* SMOKE AT ALL. IT'S *DISGUSTING*.

PUFF

COFF COFF

WHAT? *WAIT!* WHAT ARE YOU DOING? THAT'S *MY DESK!*

WHY ARE YOU PUTTING ALL THOSE BOXES ON MY DESK?! IT'S NOT A STORAGE FACILITY!

SORRY. ORDERS.

WELL YOU CAN TAKE YOUR /$%#&! ORDERS...

AND YOUR /$%#&! BOXES...

AND YOU CAN *PUT* THEM WHERE...

BELGIQUE!

COMMANDER PIPPINS?

AH! *TRÈS BIEN! EXCELLENT!* THE BOXES HAVE ARRIVED.

BUT WHAT IS ALL THIS?

WAIT...*FINIS?* THE SUPPOSED CRIMINAL ORGANIZATION? WHY DO *I* HAVE ALL THESE PAPERS?

ISN'T THIS A JOB FOR THE *CIA? INTERPOL?* THE *SÛRETÉ?*

YES. YES. AND YES.

...UT IT MAKES *DIFFERENCE.* ...ONE WANTS ...O TOUCH IT.

IT'S POLITICAL DYNAMITE, AND FRANKLY, QUITE *DANGEROUS.*

WHEN THE LAW GOES AFTER *FINIS...*

...IT'S NOT THE *TRAIL* THAT GOES COLD. IT'S THE *INVESTIGATORS.*

BY "GETTING COLD" I MEAN THEY'RE MURDERED.

YES, YES UNDERST YOU.

TWO DAYS LATER. MIDNIGHT. PARIS. *CIMETIÈRE DU PÈRE-LACHAISE,* THE MOST FAMOUS CEMETERY IN THE WORLD.

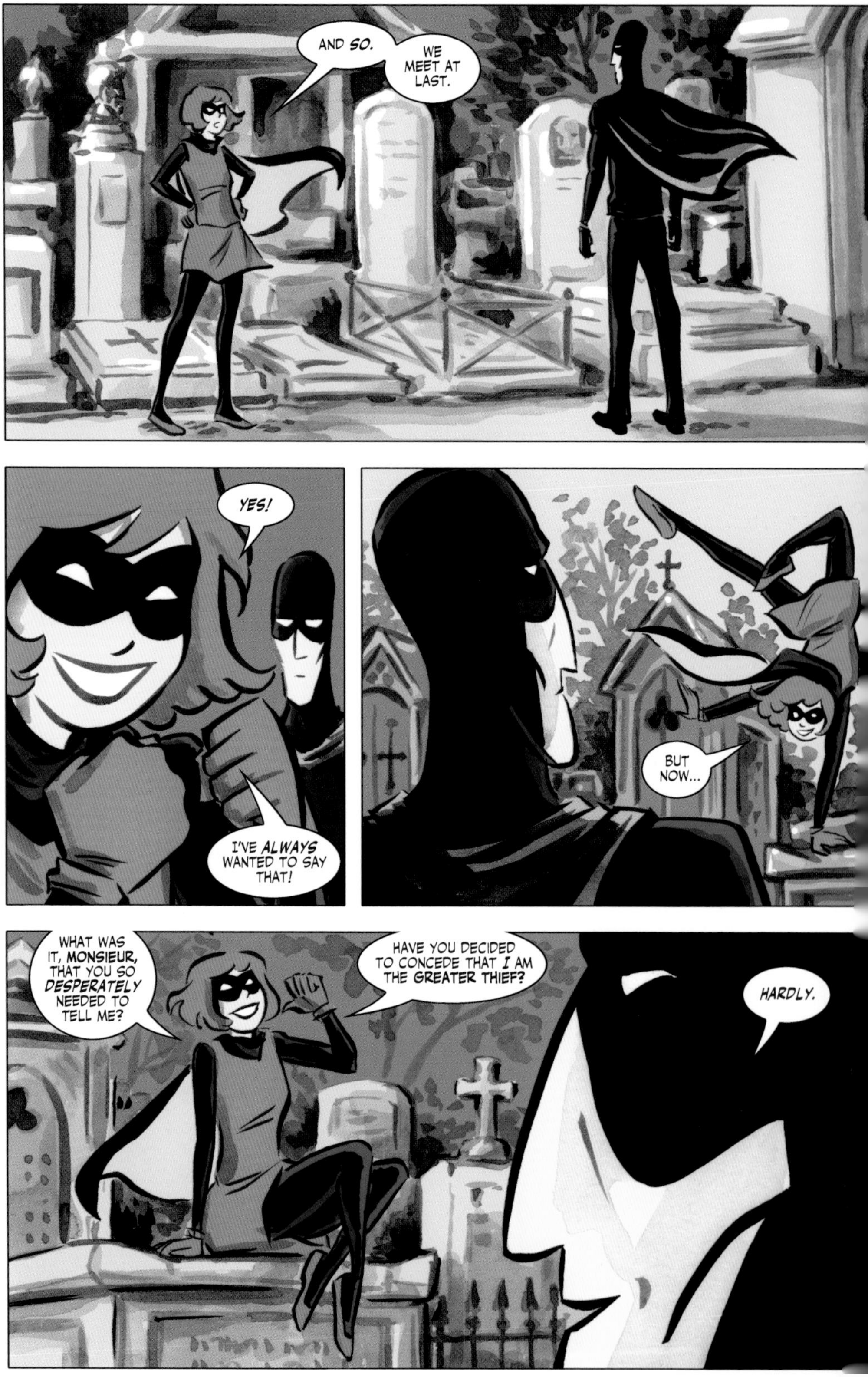
AND SO.
WE MEET AT LAST.
YES!
I'VE ALWAYS WANTED TO SAY THAT!
BUT NOW...
WHAT WAS IT, MONSIEUR, THAT YOU SO DESPERATELY NEEDED TO TELL ME?
HAVE YOU DECIDED TO CONCEDE THAT I AM THE GREATER THIEF?
HARDLY.

I ADMIT THAT YOU'RE *TALENTED*, BUT YOU LACK STYLE. *PANACHE.*

HAVE YOU GONE *MAD?* I HAVE *PRESTO!*

I, *BANDETTE*, CHALLENGE YOU TO...

SOME OTHER TIME.

FOR NOW, I ONLY WANT TO INFORM YOU...

"...WHILE ACQUIRING A CERTAIN OBJECT THE OTHER DAY, I HAPPENED TO OVERHEAR A *SPEECH* BEING DELIVERED BY *ABSINTHE.*"

ABSINTHE?

I TAKE IT YOU DON'T MEAN THE *ARTISTICALLY INEBRIATING* BEVERAGE, BUT RATHER...

THE MYSTERIOUS TRUE LEADER OF *FINIS*, CORRECT.

AND I'M AFRAID HE WANTS YOU *DEAD.*

HAH! THIS ISN'T *NEWS.* HE'S *ALWAYS* BEEN...

NO. *DON'T* DISMISS THIS.

IN THE *PAST*, HE'S CONSIDERED YOU A MERE *THORN* IN HIS SIDE.

"YOU REMEMBER THE *KILL CAPER*? AND THE *MURDER MORATORIUM*?

"*HITMAN HOLIDAY? BOMB BANDETTE?*

"...ALL PLANS BY **ABSINTHE** TO END YOUR LIFE, AND I'M AWARE OF MANY MORE. I *FOLLOW* YOUR EXPLOITS."

OUT OF *JEALOUSY?*

OUT OF *PROFESSIONALISM.* A VIRTUOSO *ALWAYS* PREPARES FOR A RIVAL.

THE POINT IS THAT *THIS* TIME, **ABSINTHE** WILL STOP AT *NOTHING.*

THE FULL RESOURCE OF *FINIS* V BE TURNE AGAINST YOU.

THE MOST *RUTHLESS KILLERS.* THE MOST *NEANDERTHAL* OF THUGS. THE *DEADLIEST* OF THEIR *ASSASSINS.* IF THEY FIND YOU...

WHAT?

THAT... LAUGH? OH *NO.*

TOO LATE, DEAR *CALF! TOO* LATE!

YOU'VE ALREADY B *FOUND.*

PÈRE-LACHAISE SHALL BE THE ARENA!

I'VE MY SWORD IN HAND!

WHO...?

I RECOGNIZE THAT VOICE.

WHAT A *FARCE*. I CAN'T BELIEVE SHE'S HERE.

WHAT YOU CAN'T BELIEVE ARE THE LETHAL SKILLS OF THE MOST FEARSOME ASSASSIN IN ALL OF *FINIS!*

DO NOT BE *DISTRACTED* BY THE *CAPE*.

FOR THE CAPE ONLY OBSCURES THE *TERRIBLE TRUTH!*

MATADORI IS HERE!

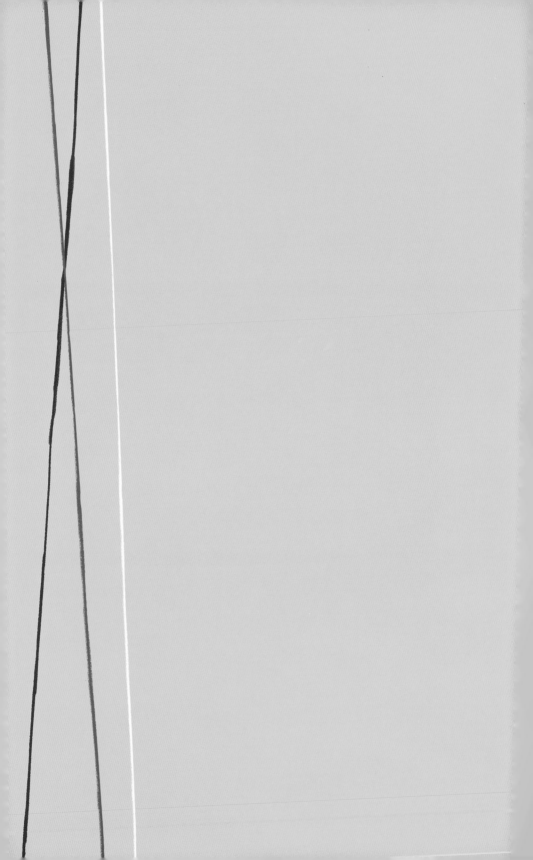

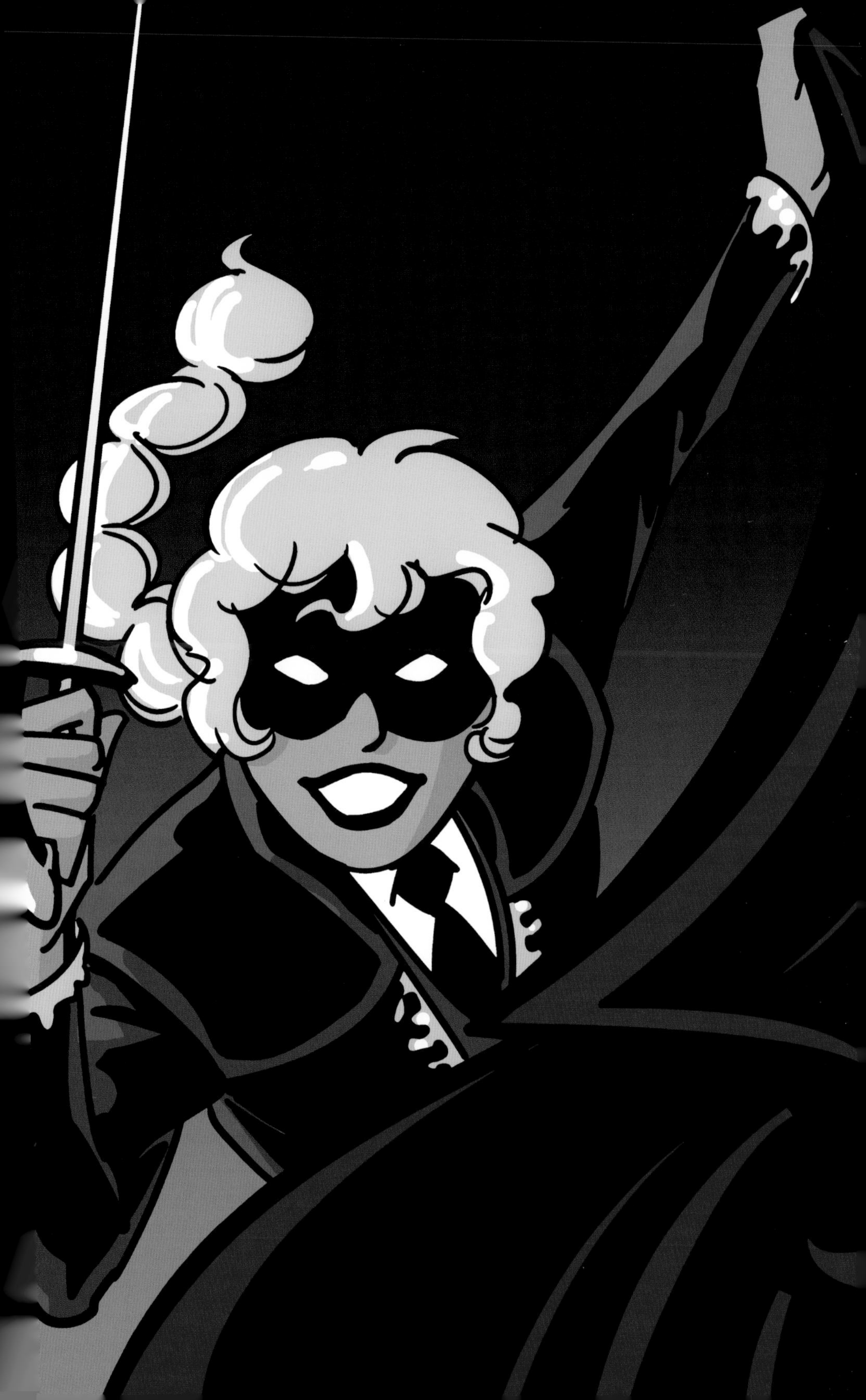

chapter four
MATADORI ENTERS THE RING!

A FIGHT?

A FIGHT!

AHH. WELL, THEN...*MONSIEUR*, PLEASE STAY BACK.

YOU ARE *OLD AND FRAIL*, AND I WOULD NOT HAVE YOU *HURT* IN THIS CLASH.

AND TADORI, FRAID YOU FIND THAT TTE IS NOT CH A *BULL* OU MIGHT WISH!

FOR WHILE A *BULL* IS A PLODDING CREATURE, I AM THE VERY *SPIRIT* OF *GRACE*!

URKK!

SERIOUSLY, I'M REALLY GOOD AT THIS STUFF.

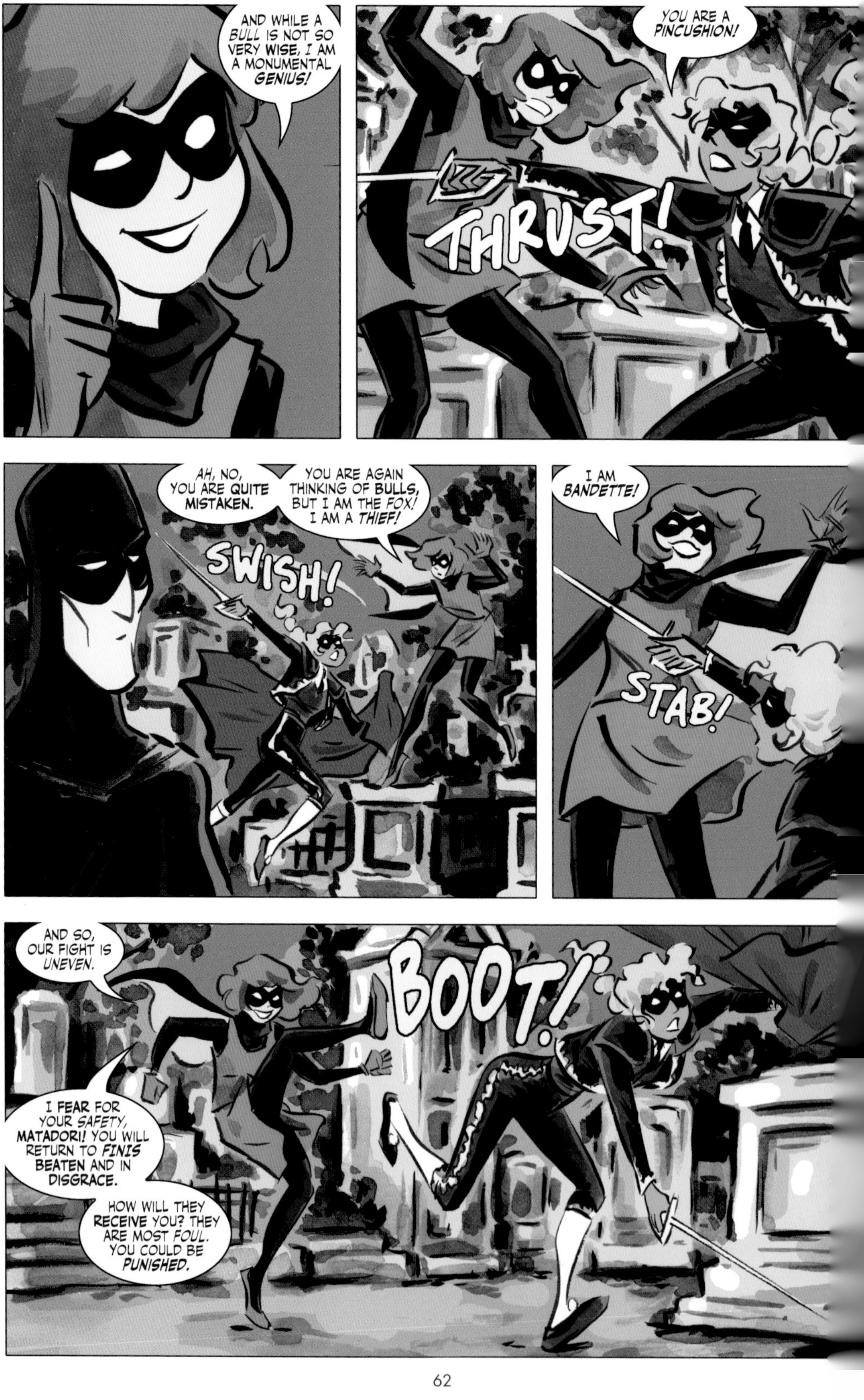
AND WHILE A BULL IS NOT SO VERY WISE, I AM A MONUMENTAL GENIUS!
YOU ARE A PINCUSHION!
THRUST!
AH, NO, YOU ARE QUITE MISTAKEN.
YOU ARE AGAIN THINKING OF BULLS, BUT I AM THE FOX! I AM A THIEF!
SWISH!
I AM BANDETTE!
STAB!
AND SO, OUR FIGHT IS UNEVEN.
BOOT!
I FEAR FOR YOUR SAFETY, MATADORI! YOU WILL RETURN TO FINIS BEATEN AND IN DISGRACE.
HOW WILL THEY RECEIVE YOU? THEY ARE MOST FOUL. YOU COULD BE PUNISHED.

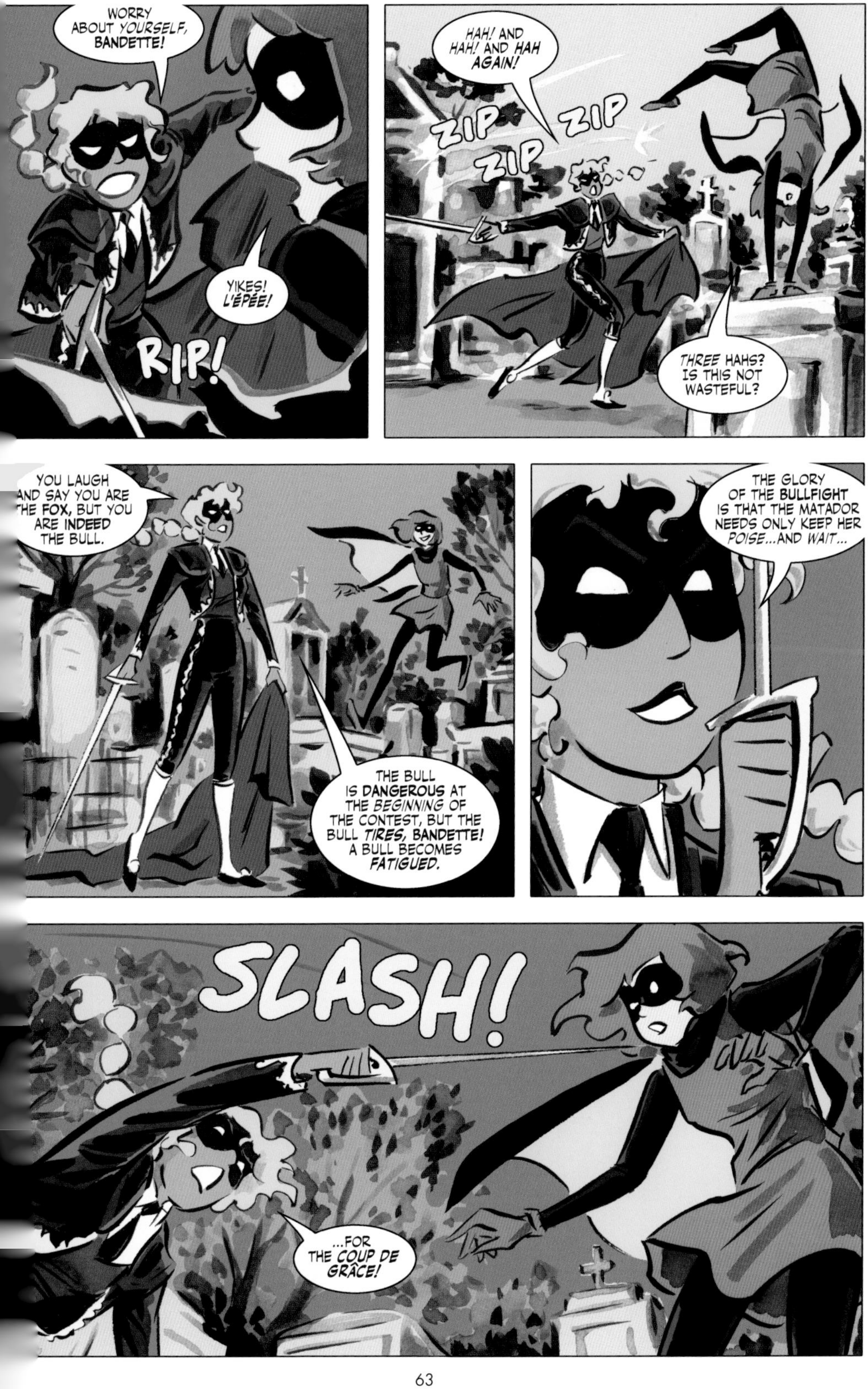
WORRY ABOUT *YOURSELF*, **BANDETTE!**
YIKES! *L'ÉPÉE!*
RIP!
HAH! AND *HAH!* AND *HAH* *AGAIN!*
ZIP ZIP ZIP
THREE HAHS? IS THIS NOT WASTEFUL?
YOU LAUGH AND SAY YOU ARE THE **FOX,** BUT YOU ARE **INDEED** THE BULL.
THE BULL IS **DANGEROUS** AT THE *BEGINNING* OF THE CONTEST, BUT THE BULL *TIRES,* **BANDETTE!** A BULL BECOMES ***FATIGUED.***
THE GLORY OF THE **BULLFIGHT** IS THAT THE MATADOR NEEDS ONLY KEEP HER *POISE*...AND *WAIT*...
SLASH!
...FOR THE *COUP DE GRÂCE!*

BAP!

CLATTER!

WAS THAT *IT*? YOUR *COUP DE GRÂCE*? WAVING YOUR *POINTY SWORD* ABOUT?

DID YOU THINK I WOULD INJURE MYSELF TRIPPING OVER YOUR *ANTICLIMAX*?

BULLFIGHTING IS FOR *BARBARIANS*, MATADORI.

SOCCER IS THE *BEAUTIFUL GAME*!

TONK!

SOCCER? HOW ABSURD!

FWEEEE

WHAT IS THE FUN OF *SOCCER*?

THE *FUN OF SOCCER*, DEAR MATADORI, IS THE *STRATEGIC CHESS GAME* OF POSITIONING FOR A *STRIKE*.

BUT THE *GLORY* OF SOCCER...

EH? BEHIND ME?

...IS THE *JOY* OF THE *PERFECT KICK*!

GOAL

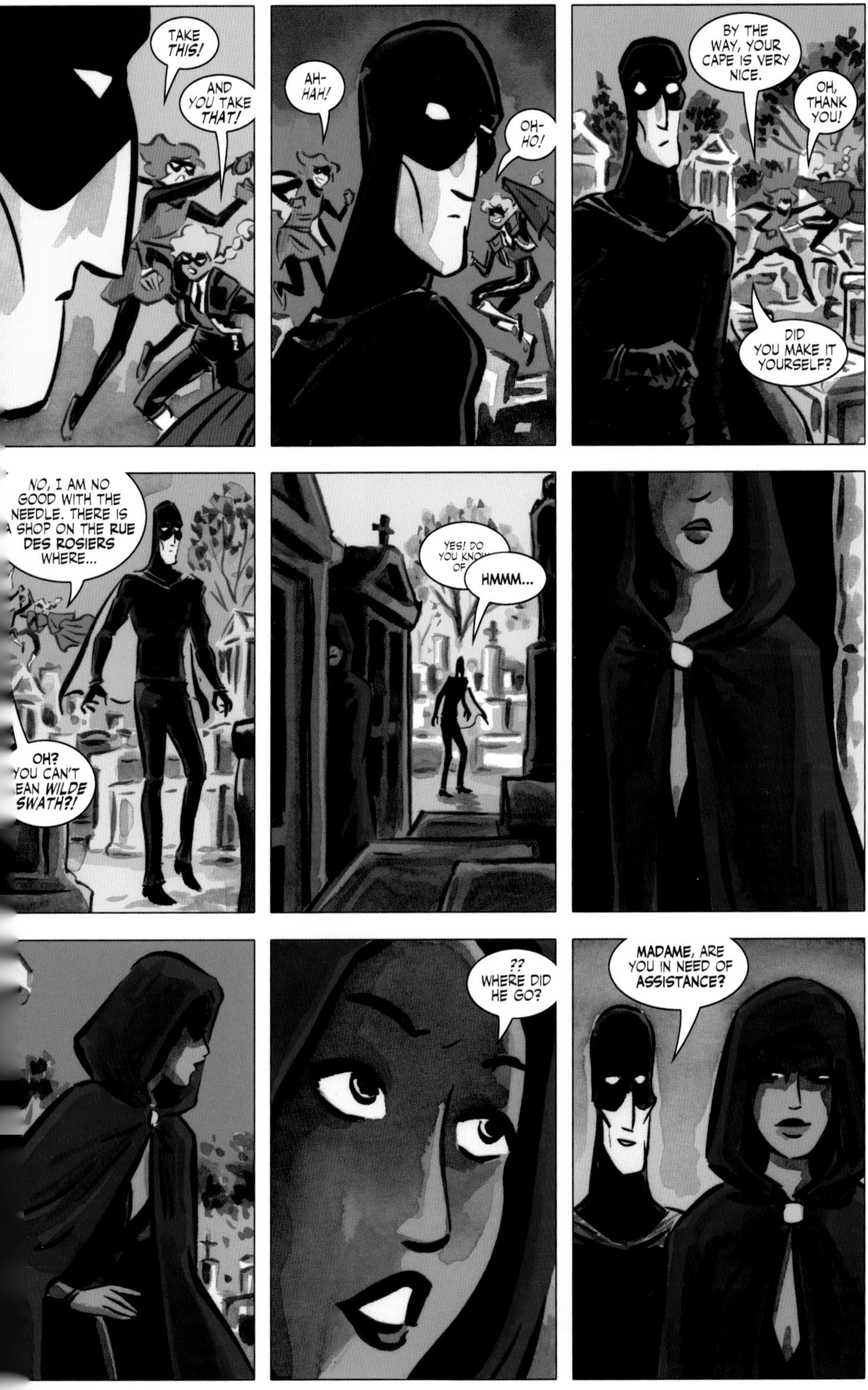
TAKE THIS!
AND YOU TAKE THAT!
AH-HAH!
OH-HO!
BY THE WAY, YOUR CAPE IS VERY NICE.
OH, THANK YOU!
DID YOU MAKE IT YOURSELF?
NO, I AM NO GOOD WITH THE NEEDLE. THERE IS A SHOP ON THE RUE DES ROSIERS WHERE...
OH? YOU CAN'T EAN WILDE SWATH?!
YES! DO YOU KNO OF
HMMM...
?? WHERE DID HE GO?
MADAME, ARE YOU IN NEED OF ASSISTANCE?

YOU'RE AS SWIFT AND SILENT AS YOUR LEGEND SUGGESTS.

AND YOU, MADAME, HAVE A FAMILIAR VOICE.

YOU ARE THE MYSTERIOUS CLIENT WHO PHONED TO HIRE ME FOR A CERTAIN *JOB*, IF I'M NOT MISTAKEN.

ARE YOU MISTAKEN OFTEN?

VERY OFTEN. BUT RARELY IN REGARDS TO A BEAUTIFUL WOMAN.

OH? DO YOU SEE ME AS A *BEAUTIFUL WOMAN*?

I SEE YOU AS AN IMPORTANT FIGURE IN A *GRAND GAME*--ONE THAT WE SHOULD BEGIN PLAYING.

WHAT IS YOUR *NAME*? WHY HAVE YOU COME HERE TONIGHT? ONLY TO *OBSERVE*?

NO, I AM RATHER MORE ACTIVE THAN THAT. I HAVE COME TO TALK ABOUT *ABSINTHE*.

YOU SPEAK OF THE *CRUEL LEADER* OF *FINIS*.

I SPEAK OF A *SCALE* THAT NEEDS TO BE *BALANCED*.

I SPEAK OF SEVEN OBJECTS THAT I WISH YOU TO STEAL.

SEVEN ARTIFACTS THAT ABSINTHE WILL MISS TERRIBLY.

YOU WISH TO HURT HIM IN THIS MANNER? HAS HE WRONGED YOU?

AND...YOU HAVE FORGOTTEN TO TELL ME YOUR *NAME*.

I ASSURE YOU, I FORGET *NOTHING*.

"FOR INSTANCE, I HAVE NOT FORGOTTEN THE LOCATION OF SEVENTY-TWO BOTTLES OF THE LEGENDARY 1871 *COMOZ ABSINTHE DES ALPES*, WHICH ABSINTHE DISCOVERED WHEN HE WAS STILL ONLY AN ASSASSIN FOR THE *UNIONE CORSE*.

"I KNOW THE RESTING PLACE OF THE ONLY COPY OF SHAKESPEARE'S LOST PLAY *CARDENIO*, WHICH ABSINTHE READ TO ME OVER THE COURSE OF TWO WEEKS IN BELGIUM.

"I REMEMBER A CERTAIN HOUSE WHICH WAS ONCE VISITED BY **VAN GOGH**, WHERE HE PAINTED THE PORTRAIT OF A WOMAN WHO HAD REFUSED TO KISS HIM.

(VAN GOGH)

"I HAVE NOT FORGOTTEN THE *SESTERTIUS OF HADRIAN* THAT ABSINTHE PAID *THREE MILLION DOLLARS* AND KILLED *FOUR MEN* TO OBTAIN."

I HAVE BROUGHT A LIST FOR YOU, MONSIEUR, OF THESE AND OTHER ITEMS, AND THEIR LOCATIONS.

I CAUTION YOU: IT IS *DANGEROUS* TO CROSS ABSINTHE.

...BUT I MUST ADMIT THAT I GIVE THIS WARNING KNOWING IT WILL ONLY *PRICK YOUR PRIDE* AND BE MET AS A CHALLENGE.

HMMM. SCENTED WITH *CARON'S POIVR* MY *FAVORITE* PERFUME.

YES. I *KNOW.*

I DID THIS TC ENSURE YOU WO REMEMBER M!

OH, AND I'M *WELL AWARE* THAT YOU *COULD* FOLLOW ME...

...THAT I COULD NEVER *HOPE* TO SHAKE OFF THE MOST TALENTED *MASCULINE* THIEF IN ALL THE WORLD...

...BUT ARE YOU *AWARE* OF HOW MANY SNIPER RIFLES *FINIS* HAS TRAINED ON YOUR YOUNG FRIEND *BANDETTE?*

YOU COULD FOLLOW *ME,* OR YOU COULD HELP *HER,* AND AT THIS MOMENT, MONSIEUR, I AM *NOT* A LADY IN DISTRESS.

WE WILL MEET AGAIN.

SPECIAL POLICE HEADQUARTERS. 12:34 AM.

PHEWWWW

INSPECTOR LOGIQUE? IS THERE ANYTHING I CAN DO FOR YOU?

EH? OH, LIEUTENANT. YOU'RE STILL HERE?

I'M YOUR ASSISTANT. UNTIL YOU GO HOME I WANT TO...I MEAN, IT'S MY DUTY TO STAY.

THEN YOU'LL BE HERE FOREVER. THE FILES ON FINIS ARE NEVER ENDING.

OH. THOSE...WOMEN. DO YOU OFTEN LOOK AT SUCH PRETTY WOMEN ON YOUR COMPUTER?

THAT'S NOT A, UMM, DATING SITE, IS IT?

YES.

...S? OH. IT'S JUST THAT, UMM, THIS MAY BE OUT OF BOUNDS, BUT...

THEY ARE ALL WOMEN WITH WHOM LENTHE, THE HEAD OF FINIS, HAS BEEN ASSOCIATED.

OH!

NEARLY ALL OF THEM ARE DEAD OR MISSING, NOW.

HEART ATTACKS. OVERDOSES. ACCIDENTS. VERY STRANGE.

OH.

AND *THIS* IS A LIST OF LAW ENFORCEMENT OFFICERS WHO HAVE LIKEWISE MET WITH ACCIDENTS.

AS YOU CAN *SEE*, THERE'S QUITE A NUMBER OF THEM.

OH, B.D....DO BE *CAREFUL.*

HMMFFF.

I BELIEVE I'LL CALL MY *MOTHER.*

NOW? AT THIS TIME OF NIGHT?

THE DRAGON NEVER SLEEPS.

AHH. *MAMA.* I'M AFRAID SOMETHING HAS COME UP. A NEW CASE. *BIG.* I MAY NOT BE ABLE TO MAKE IT FOR...

YES, YES, I *KNOW.* IT'S JUST THAT THERE'S AN ELEMENT OF *EXTREME DANGER* THAT COULD MEAN...

MAMA. *MAMA.* LISTEN TO ME. I JUST WANT YOU TO KNOW THAT, IF SOMETHING *BAD* HAPPENS, THEN...

WHAT? *NO!* THAT'S *NOT* WHAT I *SAID!* OF *COURSE* I...

SETTLE DOWN, MAMA! WHAT? *ME?* YOU'RE THE ONE WHO NEEDS TO...

THAT'S GOING *TOO* ! $@*#%$& PUT HIM ON PHONE!

$i*#&@% ß#^¢*!!

&#*$¿ǧ~$ #%&@!!

70

URK!

I BELIEVE IT IS TIME FOR YOU TO **ACKNOWLEDGE** DEFEAT.

NEVER!

I'VE ONLY BEEN **TOYING** WITH YOU!

YOU **HAVE?**

PERHAPS YOU SHOULD **NOT** DO SO. IT SEEMS PAINFUL.

YOU **DO** KNOW THAT I, **BANDETTE**, AM THE WORLD'S GREATEST THIEF, YES?

DO YOU THINK MASTER THIEVES STEAL ONLY **PAINTINGS** AND **JEWELS?** THIS IS NOT SO.

FOR EXAMPLE, WE STEAL **HEARTS** AND **SMILES,** TO GIVE TO THOSE IN **NEED.**

I HAVE ALSO STOLEN SECRET KNOWLEDGE OF MANY OF THE WORLD'S DEADLIEST MARTIAL ARTS.

JEET KUNE DO! KRAV MAGA! MUAY THAI! WITH THESE SKILLS, I CANNOT BE OVERCOME BY MERE...

HELLO?

ZEEEEEEEEN TWEEEN **CHOK!**

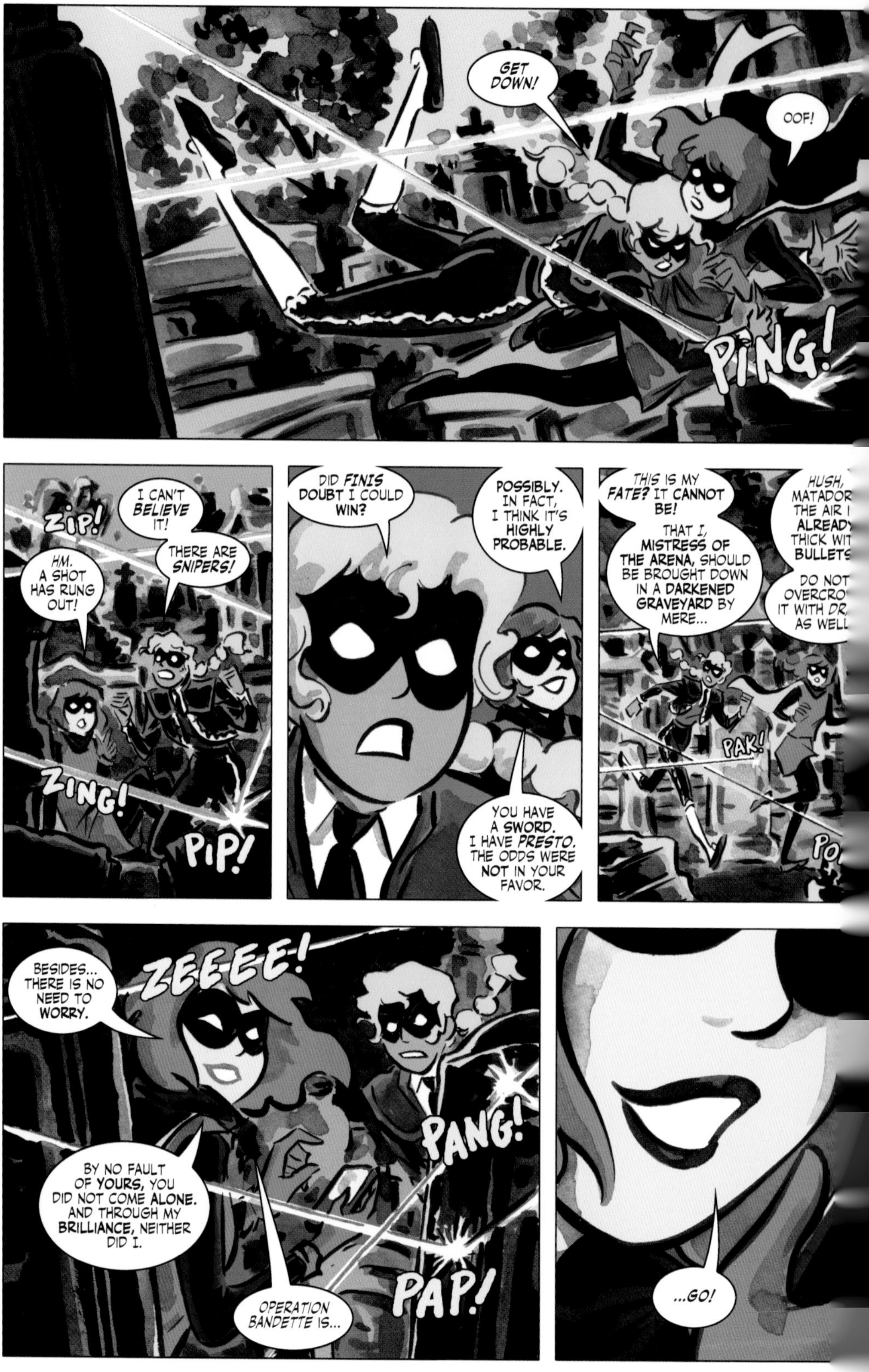
GET DOWN!
OOF!
PING!
ZIP!
I CAN'T BELIEVE IT!
THERE ARE SNIPERS!
HM. A SHOT HAS RUNG OUT!
ZING!
PIP!
DID FINIS DOUBT I COULD WIN?
POSSIBLY. IN FACT, I THINK IT'S HIGHLY PROBABLE.
YOU HAVE A SWORD. I HAVE PRESTO. THE ODDS WERE NOT IN YOUR FAVOR.
THIS IS MY FATE? IT CANNOT BE!
THAT I, MISTRESS OF THE ARENA, SHOULD BE BROUGHT DOWN IN A DARKENED GRAVEYARD BY MERE...
HUSH, MATADOR THE AIR I ALREADY THICK WIT BULLETS
DO NOT OVERCRO IT WITH DR AS WELL
PAK!
BESIDES... THERE IS NO NEED TO WORRY.
ZEEEEE!
PANG!
BY NO FAULT OF YOURS, YOU DID NOT COME ALONE. AND THROUGH MY BRILLIANCE, NEITHER DID I.
PAP!
OPERATION BANDETTE IS...
...GO!

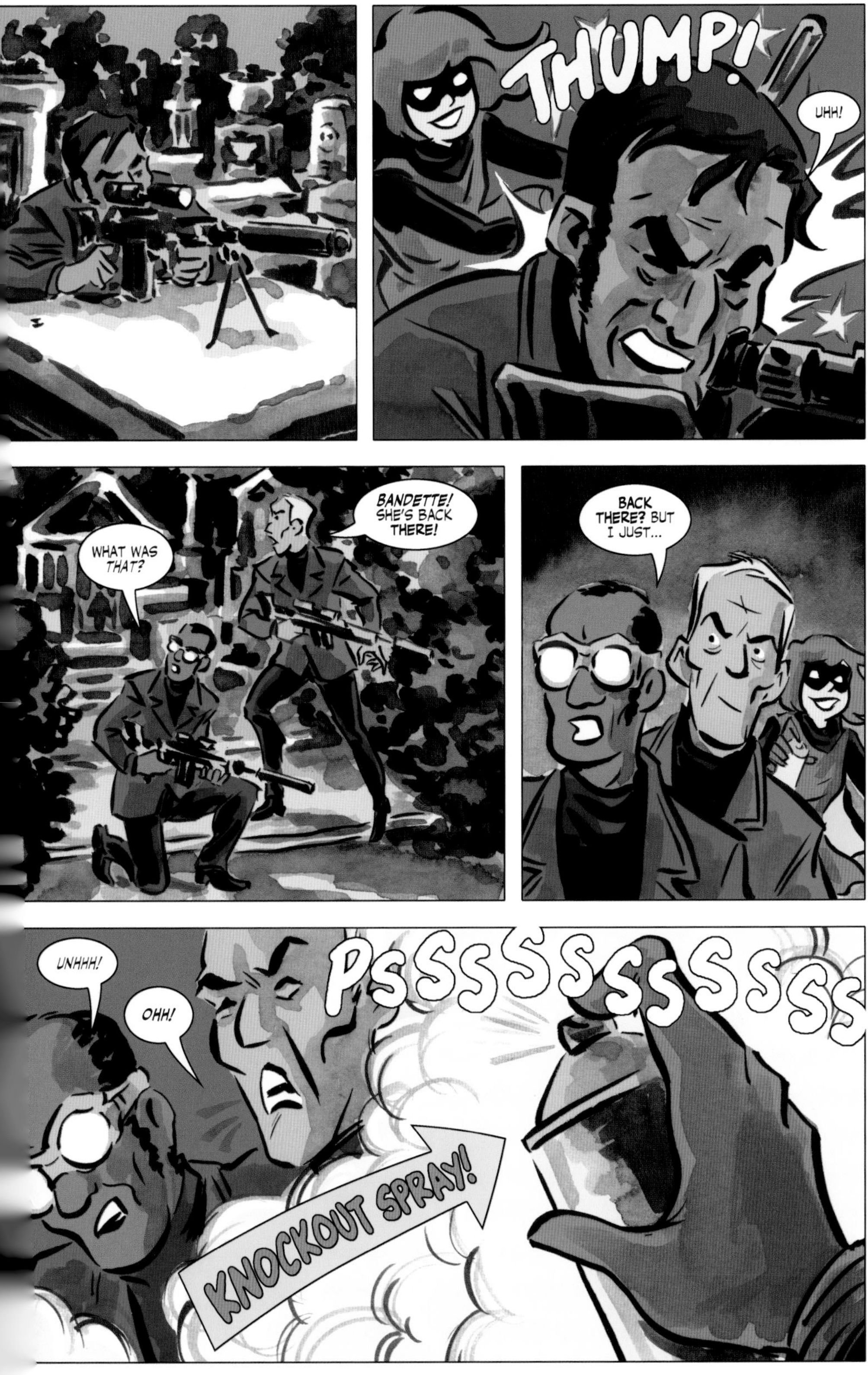
THUMP!
UHH!
WHAT WAS THAT?
BANDETTE! SHE'S BACK THERE!
BACK THERE? BUT I JUST...
UNHHH!
OHH!
PsSSSSSSSSSS
KNOCKOUT SPRAY!

WHAT'S GOING ON OVER THERE?

TOK!'

UNHH!

SHE'S HERE!

NO! SHE'S OVER HERE!

UNNHH!

OVER HERE!

PFFFSST!

HERE!

THIS IS IMPOSSIBLE!

BANDETTE IS EVERYWHERE!

BAP!

SPRAY!

HYAH

!!?

PRESTO AND PERFECTION!

I SEE I WAS NOT NEEDED AFTER ALL.

YES. IT IS TRUE. I HAD SOME ACES UP MY SLEEVE!

FRECKLES!

THE THREE BALLERINAS!

TOMMY!

PIMENTO!

YIP!

DANIEL!

THEY ARE MY URCHINS, AND WE WILL *ALWAYS* KEEP EACH OTHER SAFE.

BANDETTE, WE WILL *CONTINUE* OUR CLASH AT ANOTHER TIME.

YES, YES, OF *COURSE!* I LOOK FORWARD TO THE CLASHING.

THE *REST OF* YOU...BACK TO *HIDEOUT NUMBER SEVEN,* MY FRIENDS.

OH, AND DANIEL? YO LOOK SIMPL *RAVISHING*

AARRGH! I KNEW THAT YOU WOULD MAKE *FUN* OF...

SMEK

OH.

THERE. I DID NOT MEAN TO MAKE FUN.

COULD YOU BRING MORE CAND BARS TO TH HIDEOUT? I HAS BEEN A LONG NIGHT.

MORE BARS OF CANDY...

YOU'RE *STILL* NOT TAKING THE THREAT OF *FINIS* SERIOUSLY. TONIGHT WAS ONLY THE BEGINNING.

BAHH! IF I WISH, MONSIEUR, I DISAPPEAR.

SNAP

FINIS WIL NEVER FIND NO ONE CA UNCOVER M SECRETS.

OH? IS THAT *SO,* BANDETTE?

OR, SHOULD I SAY...

MAXIME PLOUFFE?

YES.

IT IS INDEED TRUE, MONSIEUR.

OR, SHOULD I SAY...

LEON CORVID, OF CORVID'S RARE BOOKS AND COINS?

WHAT?

BUT... HOW DID YOU...? HOW CAN...?

PRESTO.

SMEK

HA HA HA HA HA HA HA HA HA HA HA HA!!!

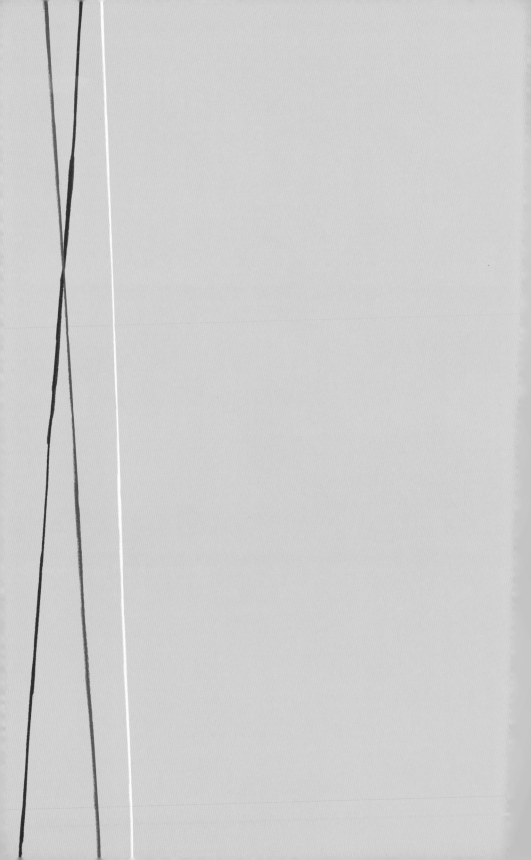

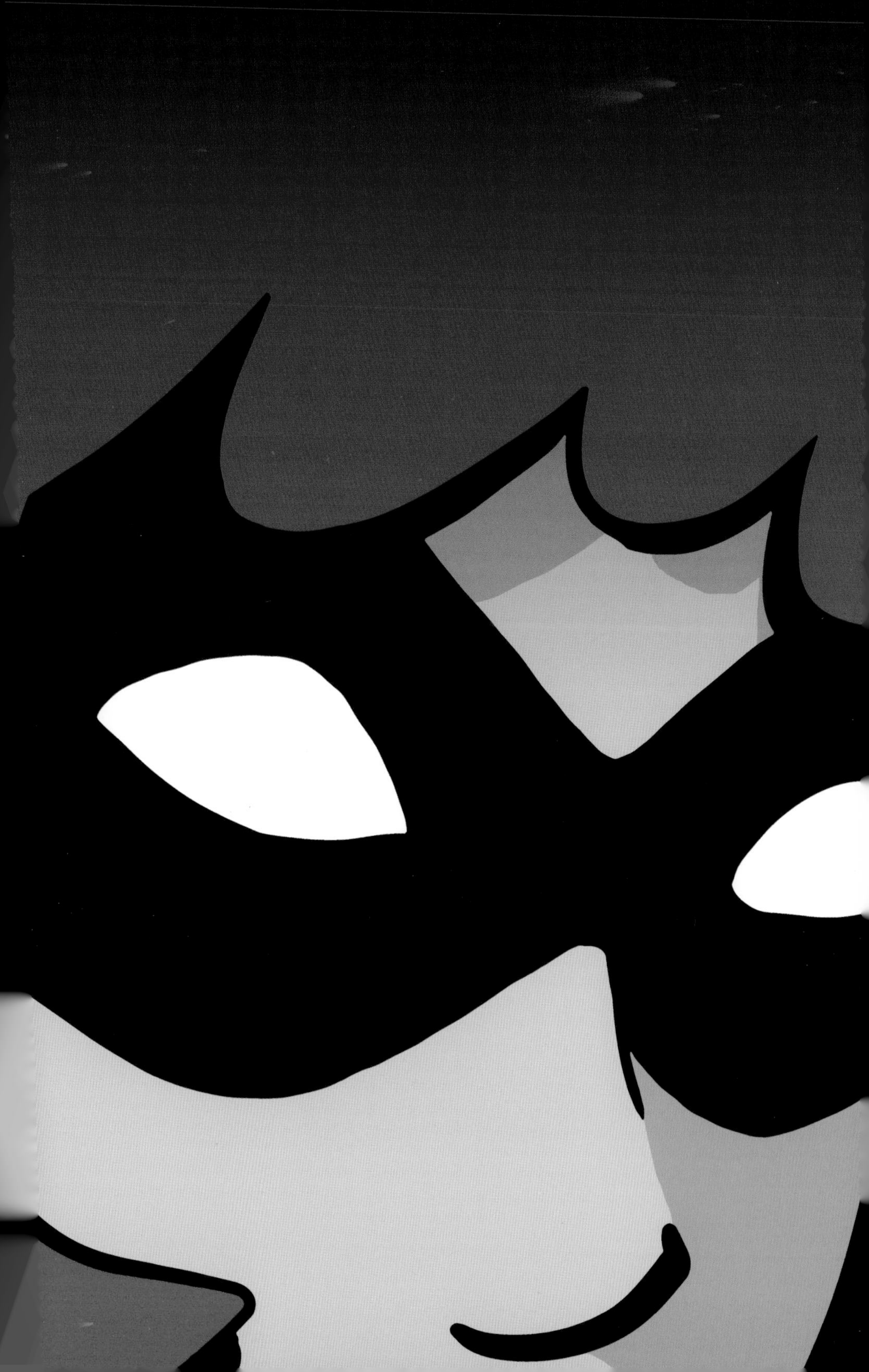

chapter five

WE WILL QUEST, NO?

HMMM.

HMMM.

KILL BANDETTE.

BUT THE *THOUGHTS,* THEY *RACE* THROUGH MY *HEAD.*

HMMM. *QUITE* A BOTHER.

Bandette
SECRET
Treasure
ROOM!

The Secret
Code is:
7-7-S-E-
F-F-A-R

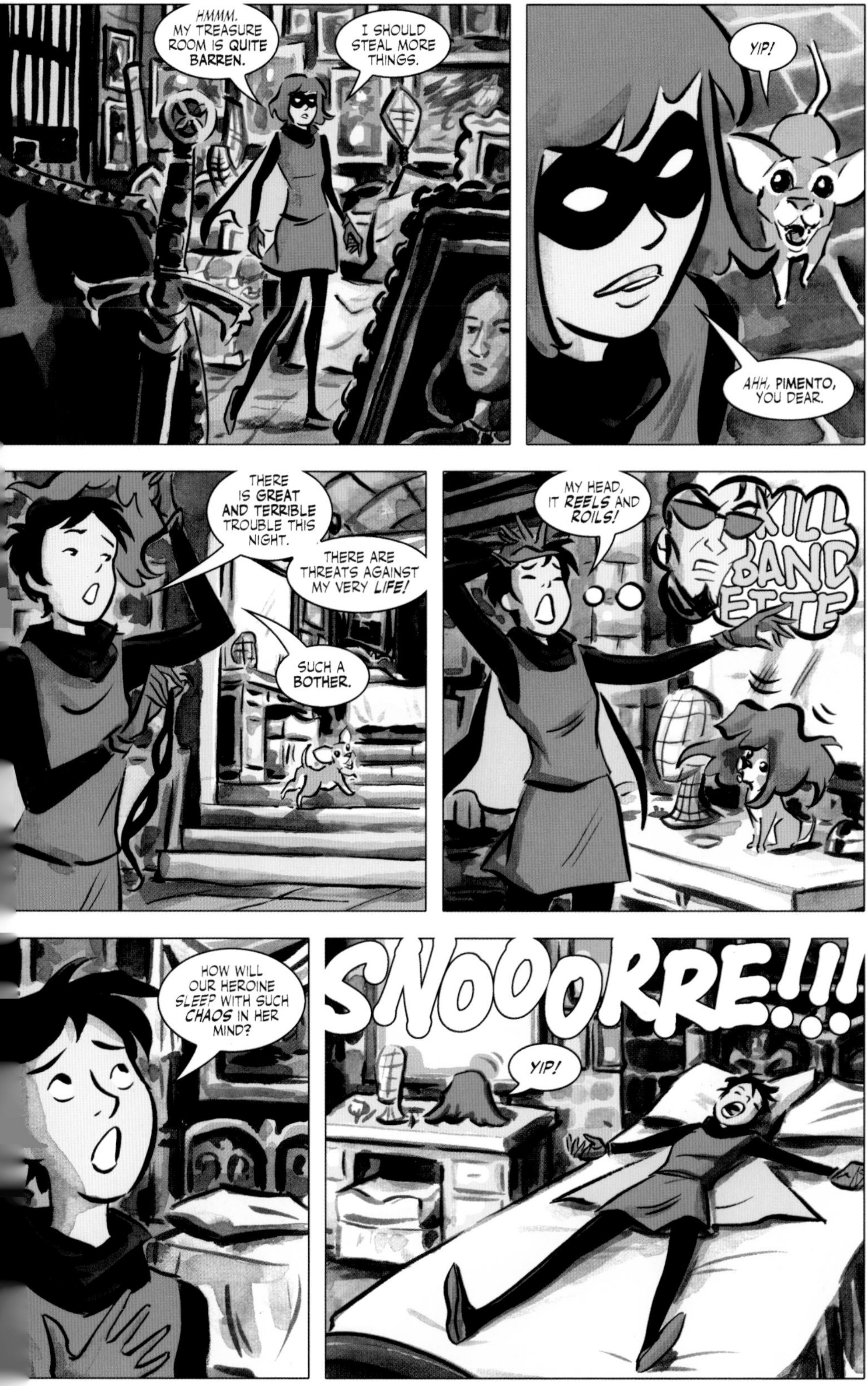
HMMM. MY TREASURE ROOM IS QUITE BARREN.
I SHOULD STEAL MORE THINGS.
YIP!
AHH, PIMENTO, YOU DEAR.
THERE IS GREAT AND TERRIBLE TROUBLE THIS NIGHT.
THERE ARE THREATS AGAINST MY VERY LIFE!
SUCH A BOTHER.
MY HEAD, IT REELS AND ROILS!
KILL BANDETTE
HOW WILL OUR HEROINE SLEEP WITH SUCH CHAOS IN HER MIND?
SNOOORRE!!!
YIP!

ELSEWHERE.

CORVID'S
RARE BOOKS
&
COINS

I HAVE BROUGHT A LIST FOR YOU, MONSIEUR.

EHH?

PAT PAT

THE LIST? WHERE IS...?

PAT

PAT
PAT
PAT

"OH. YES. YES, OF COURSE."

BANDETTE!

THE NEXT MORNING.

BUT WHAT *IS* THIS LIST?

IS IT NOT *OBVIOUS*, DANIEL? IT IS A *MISCHIEF* LIST!

A *MISCHIEF* LIST?

YES. IT'S *VERY* EXCITING!

IT'S A LISTING OF ITEMS OWNED BY *ABSINTHE*.

THEY SEEM TO BE *DEAR* TO HIM.

IT WOULD BE THE *HEIGHT* OF FOLLY TO ATTEMPT TO *STEAL* THEM.

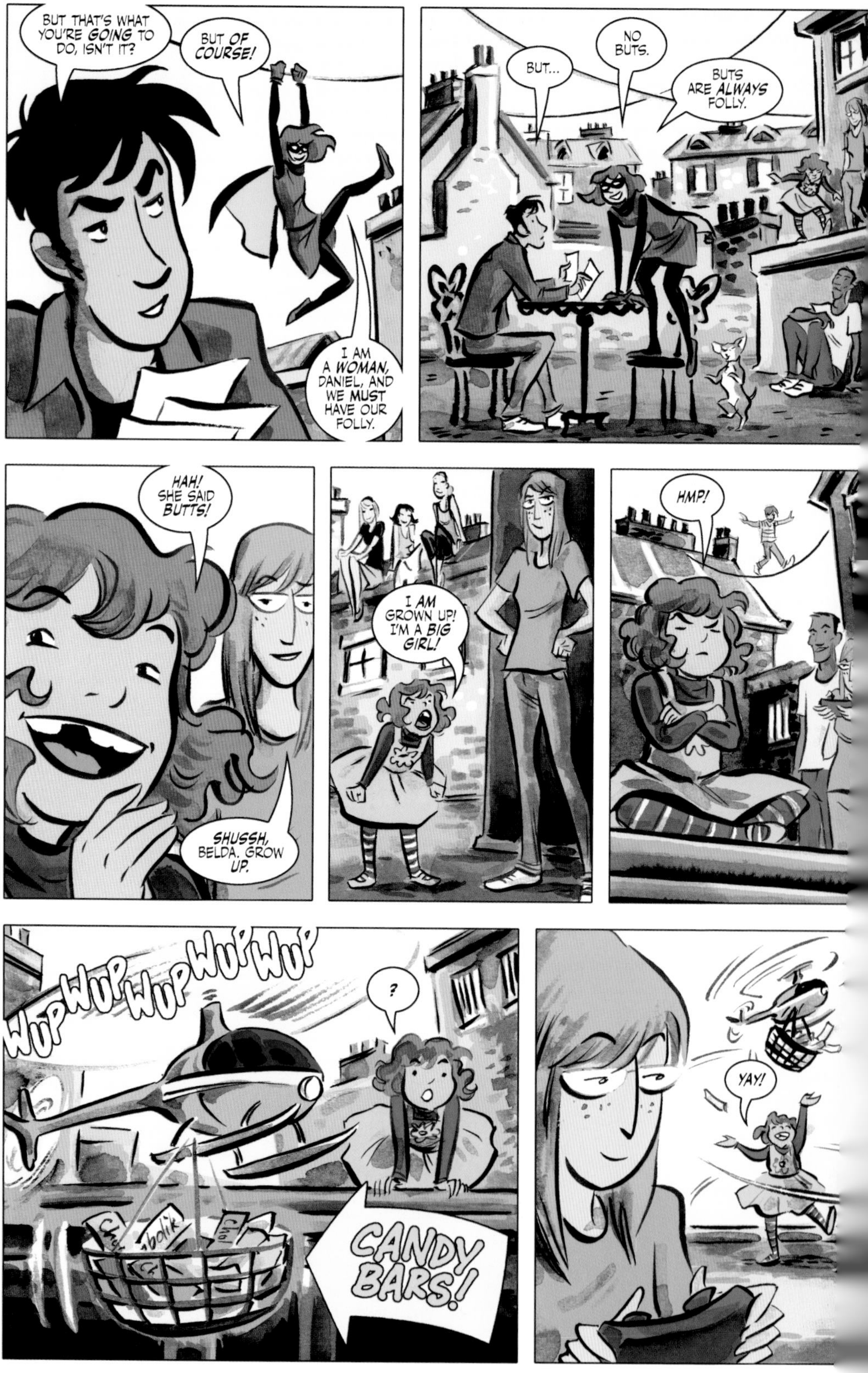
BUT THAT'S WHAT YOU'RE *GOING* TO DO, ISN'T IT?
BUT *OF COURSE!*
I AM A *WOMAN,* DANIEL, AND WE *MUST* HAVE OUR FOLLY.
BUT...
NO BUTS.
BUTS ARE *ALWAYS* FOLLY.
HAH! SHE SAID *BUTTS!*
SHUSSH, BELDA. GROW *UP.*
I *AM* GROWN UP! I'M A *BIG GIRL!*
HMP!
WUP WUP WUP WUP WUP WUP
?
CANDY BARS!
YAY!

MY POINT IS... FOLLY IS **WRONG**, BANDETTE. IT MEANS THAT--

DANIEL, IF THERE IS NOT **FOLLY** IN THE WORLD, THEN THE **WORLD ITSELF** IS FOLLY.

YOU MUST UNDERSTAND THAT **MISTAKES** ARE NOT ALWAYS **REGRETS**.

ARE THERE NOT **RASH ACTIONS** YOU LONG TO TAKE?

IS THERE NOT SOMETHING YOU WISH FOR THAT IS **BRAZEN, IMPETUOUS,** AND...**FOLLY?**

AHHH, BUT BANDETTE NOW SUPPOSES YOU WISH TO **GRAB HER UP** IN YOUR ARMS AND **KISS** HER.

BUT THAT WOULD BE *FOLLY*, DANIEL.

UHHH?

AU REVOIR, MON CHER AMI.

YIP!

GRAB!

YIP!

LEAP!

WELL, *THAT* WA RATHER A M MESSAG WASN'T

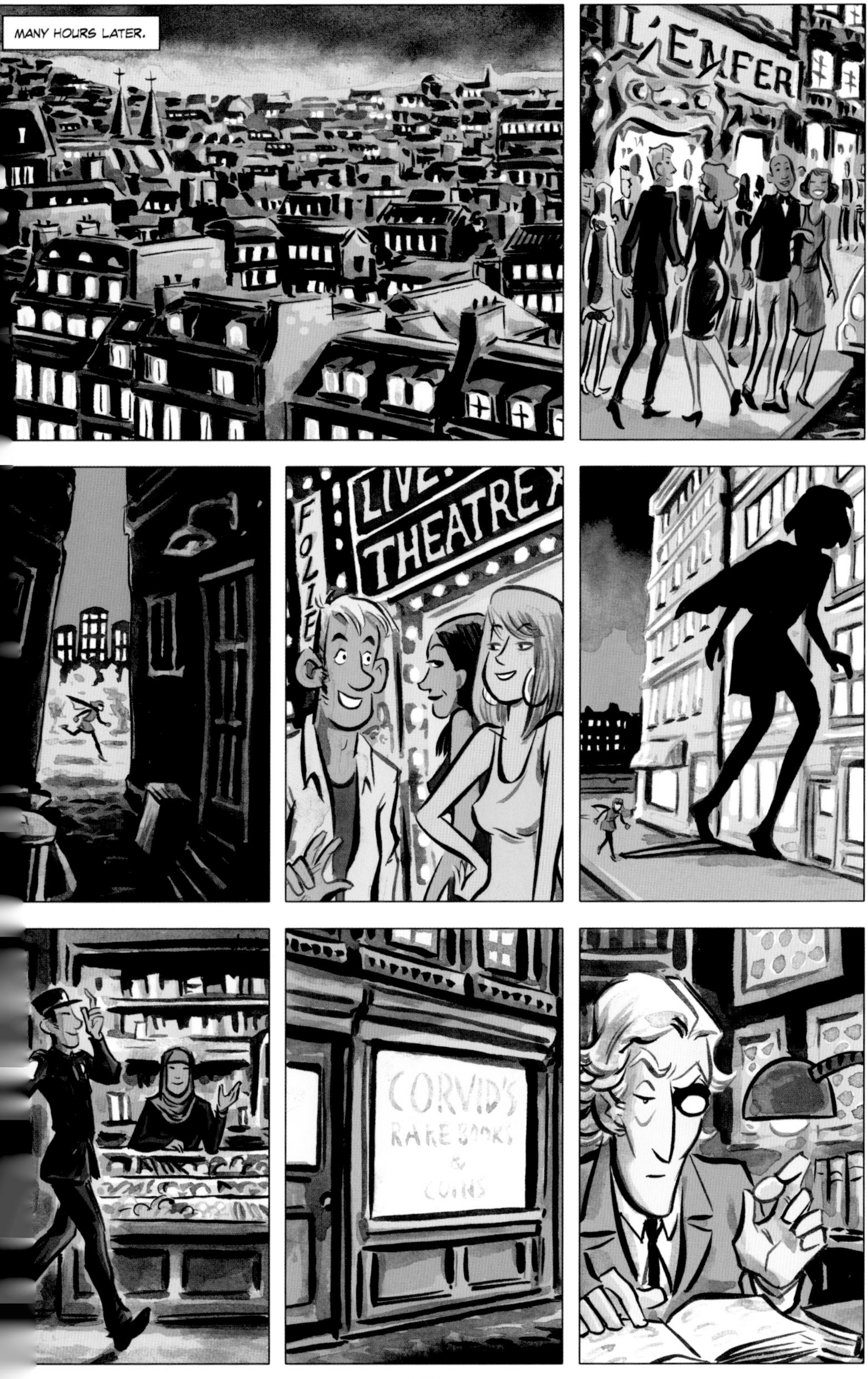
MANY HOURS LATER.
L'ENFER
LIVE
THEATRE
FOLIE
CORVID'S
RARE BOOKS
&
COINS

CREAK

SHUFFLE
SHUFFLE

EHH?

YIP.

HELLO?

YIP!

HIS NAME IS *PIMENTO*.

AH.

OH. DID I *STARTLE* YOU? SEVEN THOUSAND APOLOGIES.

THE DOOR WAS *LOCKED*, SO I LET MYSELF IN.

OF COURSE. WHY NOT?

MAY I HAVE SOME *TEA*? DO YOU HAVE COOKIES? YOU *MUST* HAVE COOKIES.

WHAT KIND OF ROGUE WOULD NOT HAVE COOKIES?

I'LL SEE WHAT I CAN FIND.

MMMM–HMMM–HM–MM.

THERE ARE BISCUITS.

BISCUITS ARE *NOT* COOKIES, BUT I SUPPOSE THEY *ARE* BISCUITS. THEY WILL HAVE TO *DO*.

INCIDENTALLY, I HAVE BROUGHT YOU YOUR *LIST*. I *STOLE* IT FROM YOU.

I KNOW. AND I STOLE IT *BACK* FROM YOU JUST NOW.

CRUNCH!

WHAT? WHY, YOU *DID!*

BUT, HOW *MAGNIFICENT!* YOU ARE AS GREAT AS YOUR *LEGEND!*

PAT PAT

AND IN FACT, BECAUSE OF YOUR TALENTS AS *MONSIEUR,* I, BANDETTE, HAVE COME TO PROPOSE A PARTNERSHIP!

BETWEEN *US?* WELL, I SUPPOSE THAT--

HAH! BETWEEN *US?* NO! SUCH A THING! DO CATS PARTNER WITH OTHER *CATS?*

NO, MONSIEUR! THIS *CANNOT* BE!

YIP!

WE ARE MADE TO *SCRATCH* AT EACH OTHER, YOU AND I.

THE PARTNERSHIP WILL BE BETWEEN EACH OF US--*INDIVIDUALLY*--AND THIS MAN: *INSPECTOR B. D. BELGIQUE.*

OF THE *SPECIAL POLICE?*

BUT OF COURSE.

YIP!

YOU AND I SHALL OBTAIN THE ITEMS ON THIS LIST, AND WE WILL DO SO PROPERLY...AS *RIVAL THIEVES.*

IT SHALL BE *MUCH* MORE FUN THAT WAY.

GRRR.

BUT...*DURING* OUR RACE FOR THESE ACQUISITIONS, WE WILL ASSUREDLY UNCOVER THE TRUTHS OF *ABSINTHE,* AND THEREFORE OF *FINIS.*

WE WILL *PROVIDE* THESE PROOFS TO THE DELIGHTFULLY NOSED *INSPECTOR BELGIQUE,* THE MAN CHARGED WITH INVESTIGATING THAT FOUL ORGANIZATION.

92

"TOGETHER, THOUGH SEPARATE, WE WILL END THE REIGN OF *ABSINTHE* AND *FINIS!*"

IN MY DEFENSE, *BANDETTE* WAS...

THAT'S *ENOUGH.*

MY DECISION, AS ALWAYS, IS *FINAL.*

MATADORI HAS *FAILED.*

TAKE HER AWAY AND SHOW HER THE PRICE OF SUCH *FOLLY.*

HEH.

!!

WHAT? BUT...

HEY!

WHAT IS THE PRICE OF HER FOLLY?

HE DIDN'T EXACTLY SAY. I THINK WE'RE SUPPOSED TO... *KILL* HER?

I DON'T THINK YOU *ARE*.

I BELIEVE YOU ARE SUPPOSED TO GIVE ME *CAKE*.

NO CAKE FOR YOU.

BANG

94

SEND HIM IN.

GEEZ, BOSS. YOU MEAN...?

YES.

HIM.

WE SHALL SEE IF BANDETTE CAN SURVIVE THIS.

WE BOTH HAVE OUR COPIES OF THE *LIST*, YES?

YES.

THEN I DECLARE THE GREAT THIEVING RACE TO B: *UNDERWAY!*

GO!

NEXT: STEALER: KEEPERS!

Illustration by Steve Lieber

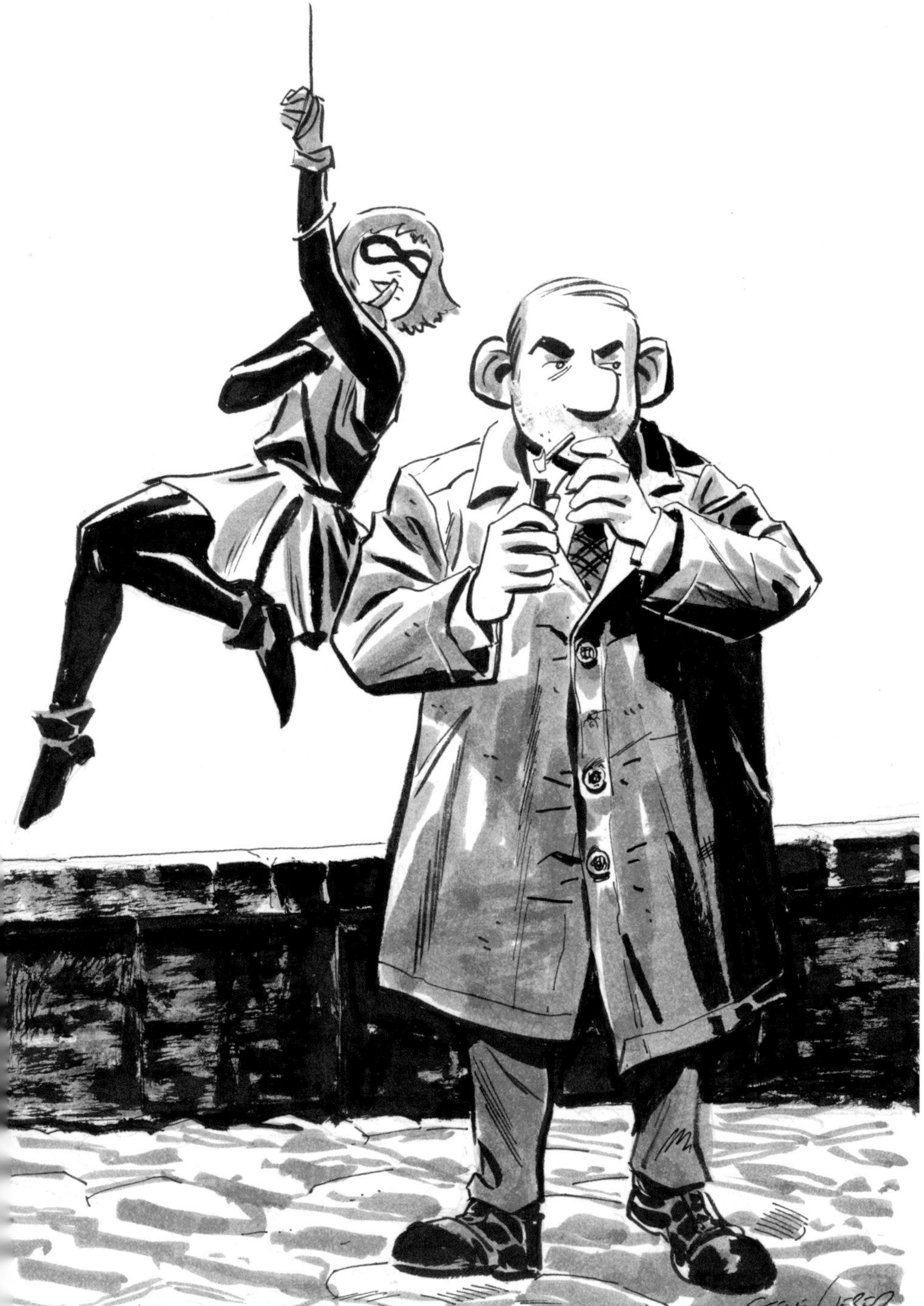
STEVE LIEBER

URCHIN STORIES

Written by Paul Tobin

B.D. BELGIQUE in SIGNS

BY PAUL TOBIN & STEVE LIEBER

BANDETTE CREATED BY PAUL TOBIN & COLLEEN COOVER

...AND IT IS *ONLY* BECAUSE YOU'VE *HELPED* US IN THE ⋛*COUGH COUGH*⋚ PAST, OR ELSE THE FULL ⋛*COUGH COUGH*⋚ FORCE OF THE LAW WOULD BE ON YOUR TRAIL, BANDETTE.

HOW *DIRE! ALAS!* I SHIVER IN *FEAR*.

AND *YOU* SHIVER WITH COUGHS, MY DEAR POLICEMAN. IT IS TIME TO GIVE UP THE CLAYMORE CIGARETTES, *NO?*

ND THEY'RE MORES. NOT YMORES.

AND THERE'S *NO* REASON TO QUIT.

NO REASON? *QUELLE IDIOTE!* WAS IT NOT A *SIGN...*

...WHEN YOU *FAILED* TO CATCH ME DURING THE *VERMEER'S KITTEN CAPER?*

HAHAHA HAHA

COUGH COUGH

MEW

MEW

MEW! PERT?

AND WAS IT NOT A *SIGN* TO QUIT YOUR CRAVE-MORE CIGARETTES AFTER YOU FAILED TO CATCH ME AT THE CULMINATION OF THE *HIGH-WIRE HEIST?*

HAHAHAHA HA HA HA

COUGH! COUGH!

YOU'RE A *MASTER* THIEF, BANDETTE. BUT *YOUNG.* YOU CAN'T TELL THE DIFFERENCE BETWEEN MERE *HAPPENSTANCE* AND A *SIGN.*

STOP

AHHH, B.D., BUT AS IT *HAPPENS* MY *STANCE* IS MERELY THAT I BELIEVE *SIGNS* ARE ALL AROUND US!

PACK OF CRAYMORES, PLEASE.

AHH, *INSPECTOR BELGIQUE!* YOU'RE IN *LUCK.* IT'S MY *LAST* PACK.

HAND OVER ALL YOUR *MONEY!* AND *GIMME* THAT PACK OF *CRAYMORES!*

TOK

IS EVERYTHING OKAY, B.D.? I'VE HEARD AN ODD NOISE.

AHHH, NOTHING, BANDETTE. IT WAS *NOTHING* AT ALL. ONLY SOMEONE *ELSE* BELIEVING IN SIGNS.

STOP

THE

100

THE MYSTERY OF MONSIEUR!

STORY:
PAUL TOBIN
ART:
ALBERTO J.
ALBURQUERQUE

WHO IS THE ENIGMATIC FIGURE KNOWN AS *MONSIEUR?* WHO IS THE MAN SHROUDED BOTH BY A MASK, AND BY *DECADES* OF MYSTERY?

WE GO TO THE **MAN** ON THE STREET TO ANSWER THIS AND MANY *OTHER* QUESTIONS.

WHAT DO YOU THINK IS MONSIEUR'S *GREATEST CAPER?*

UM, THE VAN GOGH BRUSH THEFT?

WRONG! IT WAS WHEN HE STOLE THE *DOWAGER'S DARK DIAMONDS!*

NO! THE DA VINCI DANCE!

OH, THAT *WAS GOOD!* BUT NO MATCH FOR *GOLDEN SWAN DIVE!*

HE STOLE MY HEART! MY HEART!

NO! HIS GREATEST THEFT WAS...

"...THE FRENCH COURTESAN'S TASSELS!"

"OR RASPUTIN'S PRIVATE HOARD OF *1872 LE BAISER VERT ABSINTHE.*"

GOOD ANSWERS, ALL.

NOW THEN, **WHERE DO YOU** THINK MONSIEUR CAME FROM? WHO **IS** THE MYSTERY MAN?

AHHHHHHHHHHHHHHHHHHH...

I THINK HIS MOTHER WAS A SORCERESS.

A SORCERESS? THAT'S STUPID! NO, THE TRUTH IS...

"...MONSIEUR SPRANG OUT FROM PANDORA'S BOX, LIKE VENUS FROM THE SEA."

THAT'S DUMB. EVERYONE KNOWS MONSIEUR IS THE ONLY FRENCH NINJA.

HUH? WRONG! MONSIEUR IS THE PERSONIFICATION OF THEFT.

"WHAT ARES WAS TO WAR, MONSIEUR IS TO BURGLARY."

THEN YOU THINK MONSIEUR IS THE GREATEST OF THIEVES?

YES.

YES.

WELL...

DEFINITELY MONSIEUR! CHECK IT OUT! I MADE THIS SHIRT!

I WENT TO THE LOUVRE AND ALL I GOT WAS THIS SHIRT AND A LOT OF THINGS I STOLE

MONSIEUR? PIFFLE!

HIM? THE GREATEST THIEF?

C'EST SACRILÈGE!

HMMM. MORE DISAGREEMENT.

HAVE WE DISAGREED?

THERE IS NO DISAGREEMENT!

NOUS SOMMES D'ACCORD!

102

BUT WHAT IS MONSIEUR'S FAVORITE *DRINK*?

COGNAC.

COGNAC.

YES. COGNAC.

ABSOLUTELY. COGNAC.

COGNAC.

COGNAC.

COGNAC.

YES. A COGNAC FRAPIN CUVEE 1888, IF I REMEMBER CORRECTLY.

YIP!

COGNAC.

COGNAC.

COGNAC.

SO EVERYONE IN AGREEMENT, THEN? HOW *MARVELOUS!*

EXCUSE ME.

AHHH, COGNAC.

THE END

A HINT FROM HELOISE

BY PAUL TOBIN AND TINA KIM

BANDETTE CREATED BY PAUL TOBIN AND COLLEEN COOVER

AND... 6:12 A.M.

YOU ARE *UNDER ARREST!*

AND... 6:28 A.M.

PUSH, DEAR! PUSH!

AND... 6:42 A.M.

PUT THAT *BACK!*

OH, *POO!* I AM SAYING *"POO!"*

AND... 6:53 A.M.

HERE IS YOUR COFFEE, INSPECTOR BELGIQUE.

PFF. GOOD. 'RY GOOD.

YOU KNOW, HELOISE... I CAN ALWAYS COUNT ON MY *CRAYMORE* CIGARETTES, A CLASSIC *VOLKSWAGEN,* AND *YOU...* BRINGING ME A *PERFECT* COFFEE EVERY MORNING.

AND THAT'S NICE.

THE END?

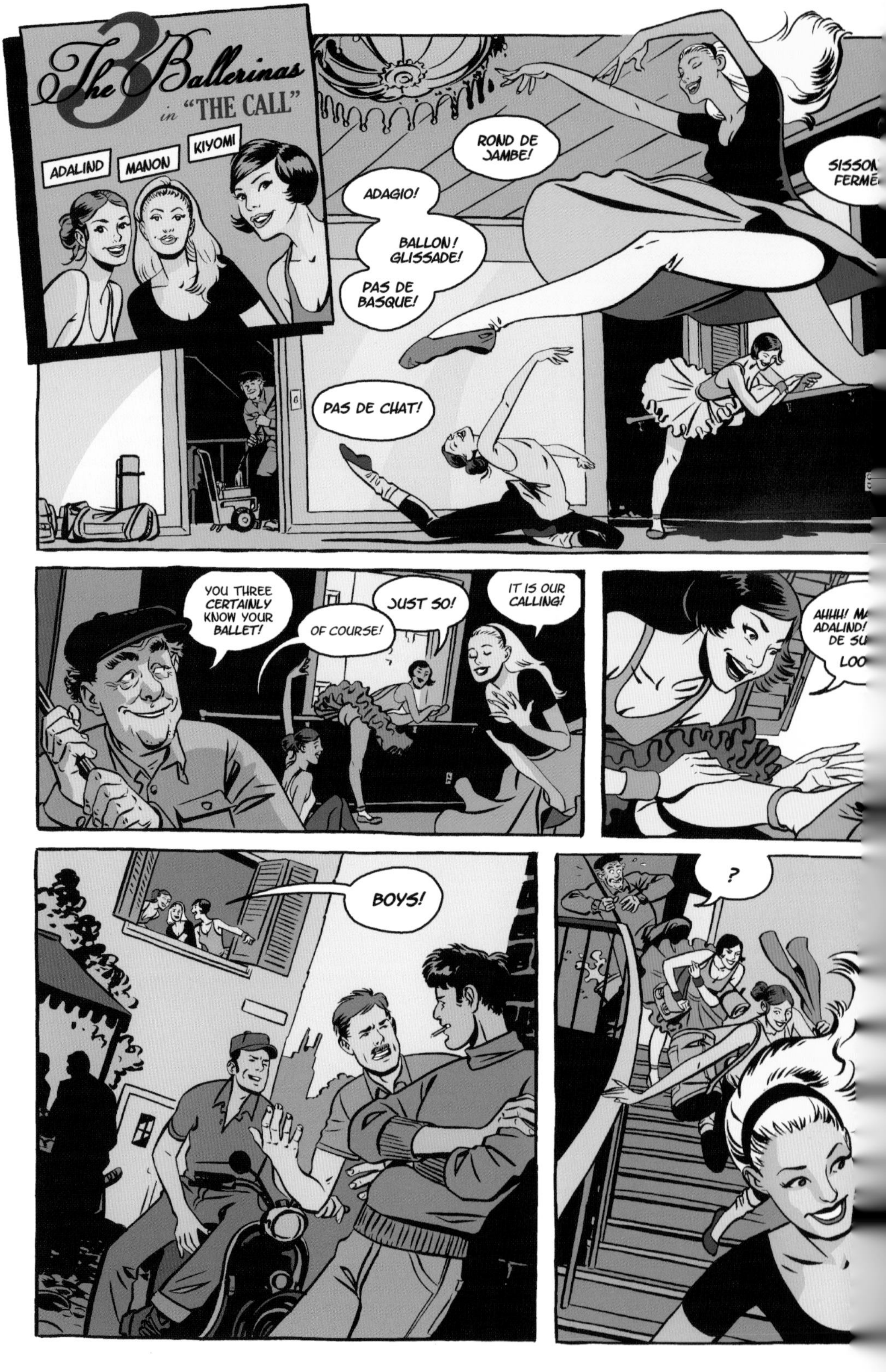
The 3 Ballerinas
in "THE CALL"
ADALIND
MANON
KIYOMI
ADAGIO!
BALLON! GLISSADE!
PAS DE BASQUE!
ROND DE JAMBE!
SISSON FERMÉ
PAS DE CHAT!
YOU THREE CERTAINLY KNOW YOUR BALLET!
OF COURSE!
JUST SO!
IT IS OUR CALLING!
AHHH! MA
ADALIND!
DE SU
LOO
BOYS!
?

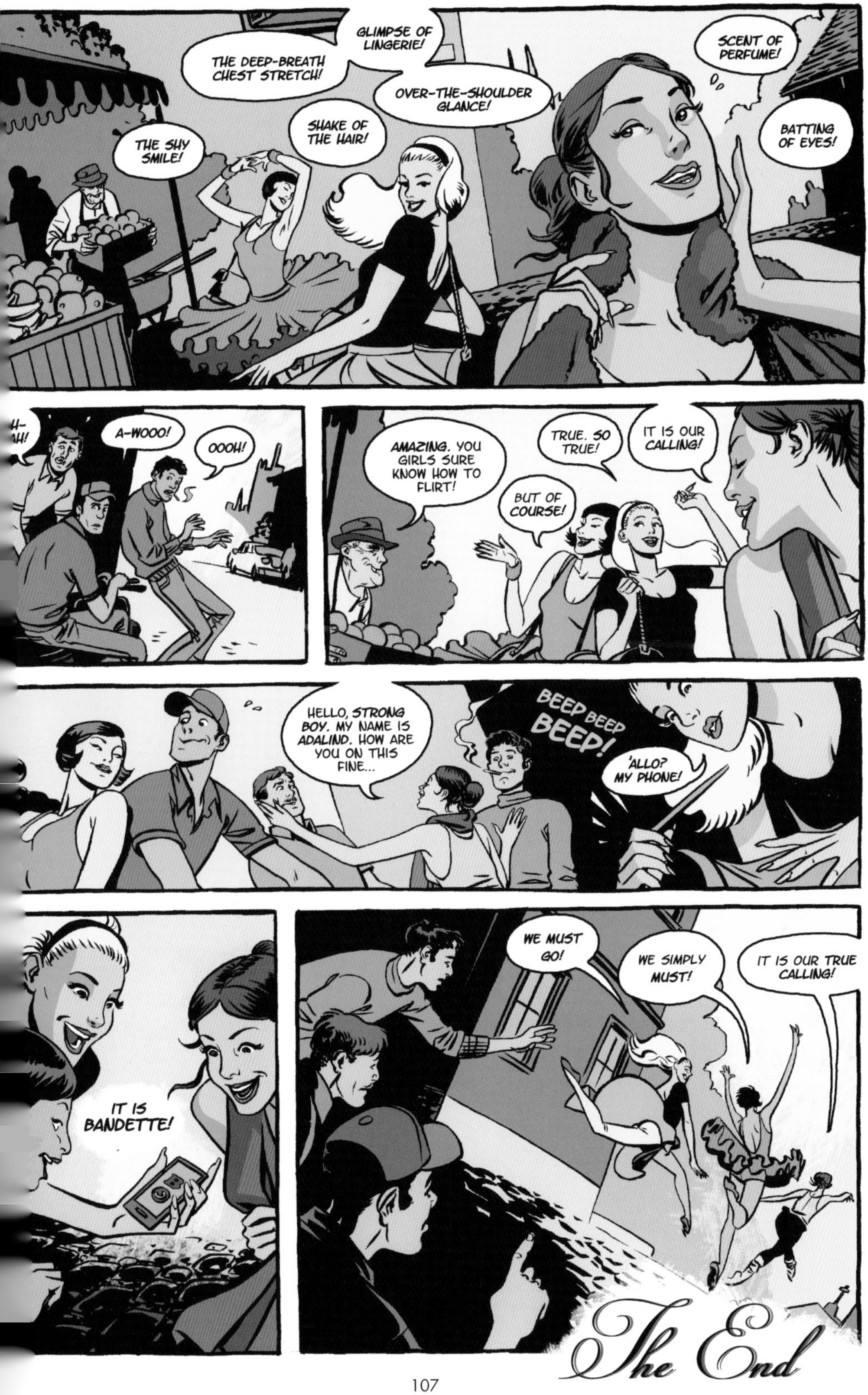
THE SHY SMILE!
THE DEEP-BREATH CHEST STRETCH!
SHAKE OF THE HAIR!
GLIMPSE OF LINGERIE!
OVER-THE-SHOULDER GLANCE!
SCENT OF PERFUME!
BATTING OF EYES!
A-WOOO!
OOOH!
AMAZING. YOU GIRLS SURE KNOW HOW TO FLIRT!
BUT OF COURSE!
TRUE. SO TRUE!
IT IS OUR CALLING!
HELLO, STRONG BOY. MY NAME IS ADALIND. HOW ARE YOU ON THIS FINE...
BEEP BEEP BEEP!
'ALLO? MY PHONE!
IT IS BANDETTE!
WE MUST GO!
WE SIMPLY MUST!
IT IS OUR TRUE CALLING!
The End

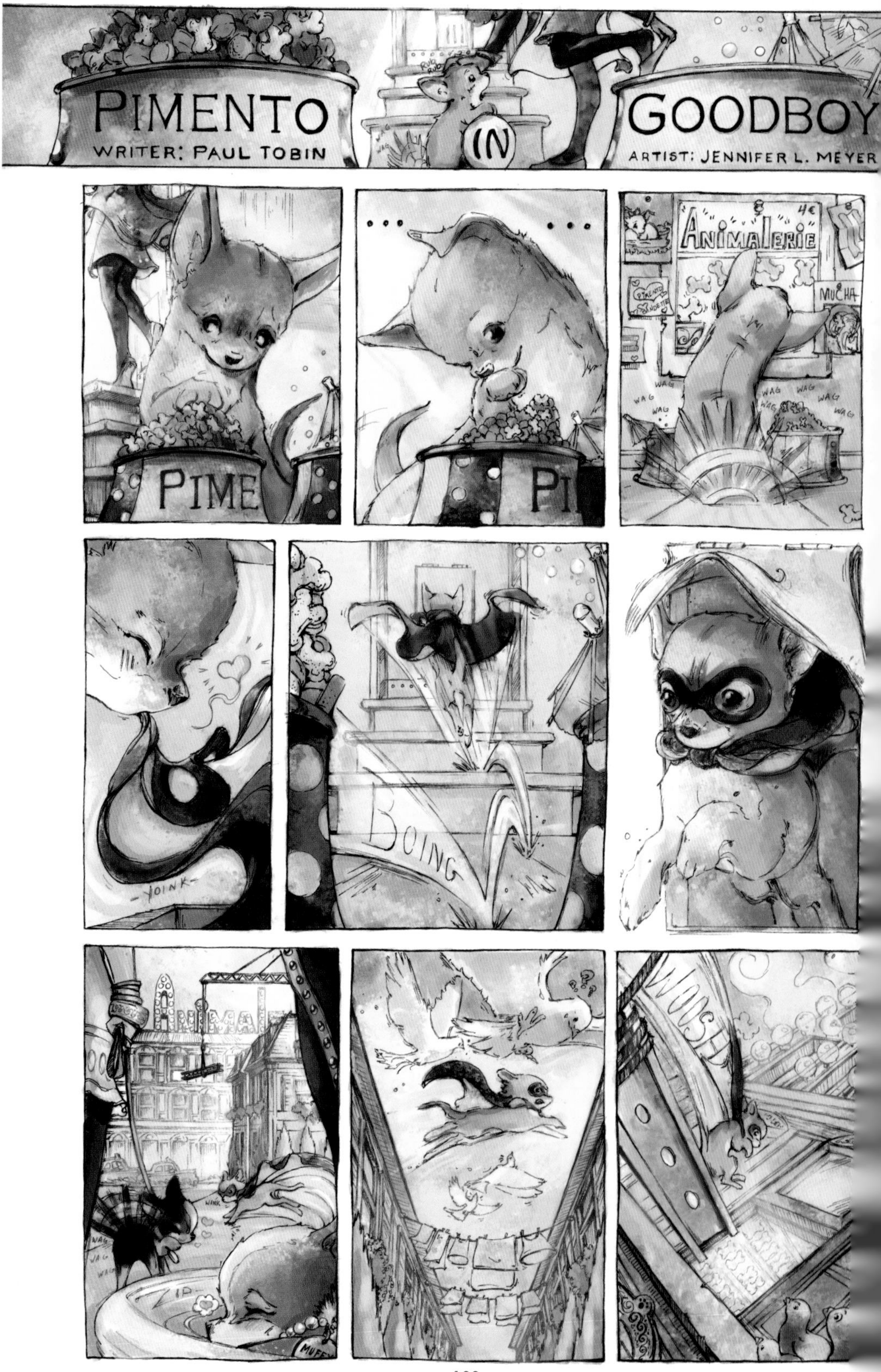
PIMENTO
IN
GOODBOY
WRITER: PAUL TOBIN
ARTIST: JENNIFER L. MEYER
PIME
...
...
PI
ANIMALERIE
4€
MUCHA
WAG WAG WAG WAG WAG WAG
YOINK
BOING
WINK
WAG WAG WAG
ZIP

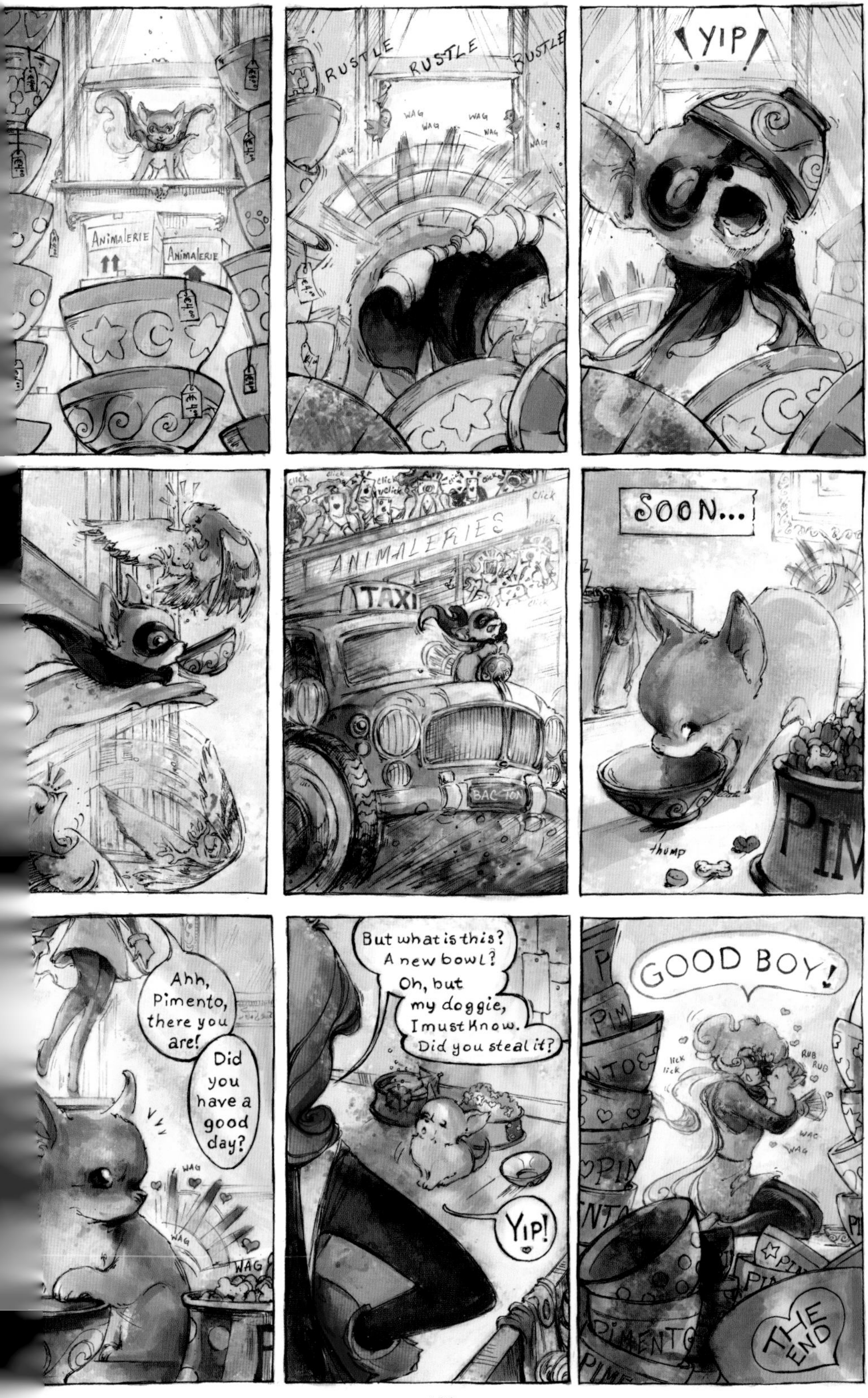

Animalerie
Animalerie
RUSTLE
RUSTLE
RUSTLE
WAG
WAG
WAG
WAG
WAG
WAG
YIP!
ANIMALERIES
TAXI
BAC-TON
SOON...
thump
PIM
Ahh, Pimento, there you are!
Did you have a good day?
WAG
WAG
WAG
But what is this? A new bowl? Oh, but my doggie, I must know. Did you steal it?
Yip!
GOOD BOY!
lick lick
RUB RUB
WAG WAG
THE END

MONSIEUR
IN: "THE LOOKING GLASS"

WORDS BY:
PAUL TOBIN

ART BY:
RICH ELLIS

BANDETTE CREATED BY:
COLLEEN COOVER AND
PAUL TOBIN

"ONE THING WAS CERTAIN, THAT THE WHITE KITTEN HAD HAD NOTHING TO DO WITH IT:-- IT WAS THE BLACK KITTEN'S FAULT ENTIERLY."

FOR THE WHITE KITTEN...HAD...HAD BEEN HAVING ITS FACE WASHED BY THE OLD CAT FOR THE LAST... UHH...

...QUARTER OF AN HOUR (AND BEARING IT PRETTY WELL, CONSIDERING): SO YOU SEE THAT IT COULDN'T HAVE HAD ANY HAND IN THE... IN THE MISCHIEF.

ARE YOU HAVEING DIFFICULTY *READING*, LILLI?

A LITTLE, LEON. I'VE GONE AND FORGOTTEN MY READING GLASSES AT WORK. IT'S A BIT OF A STRUGGLE FOR ME TO SEE THE WORDS WITHOUT THEM.

OH. PERHAPS WE SHOULD WAIT FOR ANOTHER TIME?

I'M AFRAID SO. WHAT A *BOTHER*. EVER SINCE YOU MOVED NEXT DOOR, I *SO* LOOK FORWARD TO OUR READING NIGHTS.

WHAT WITH MY *GRANDCHILDREN* THINKING THEY ARE TOO OLD FOR STORIES, I MISS...

RING
RING

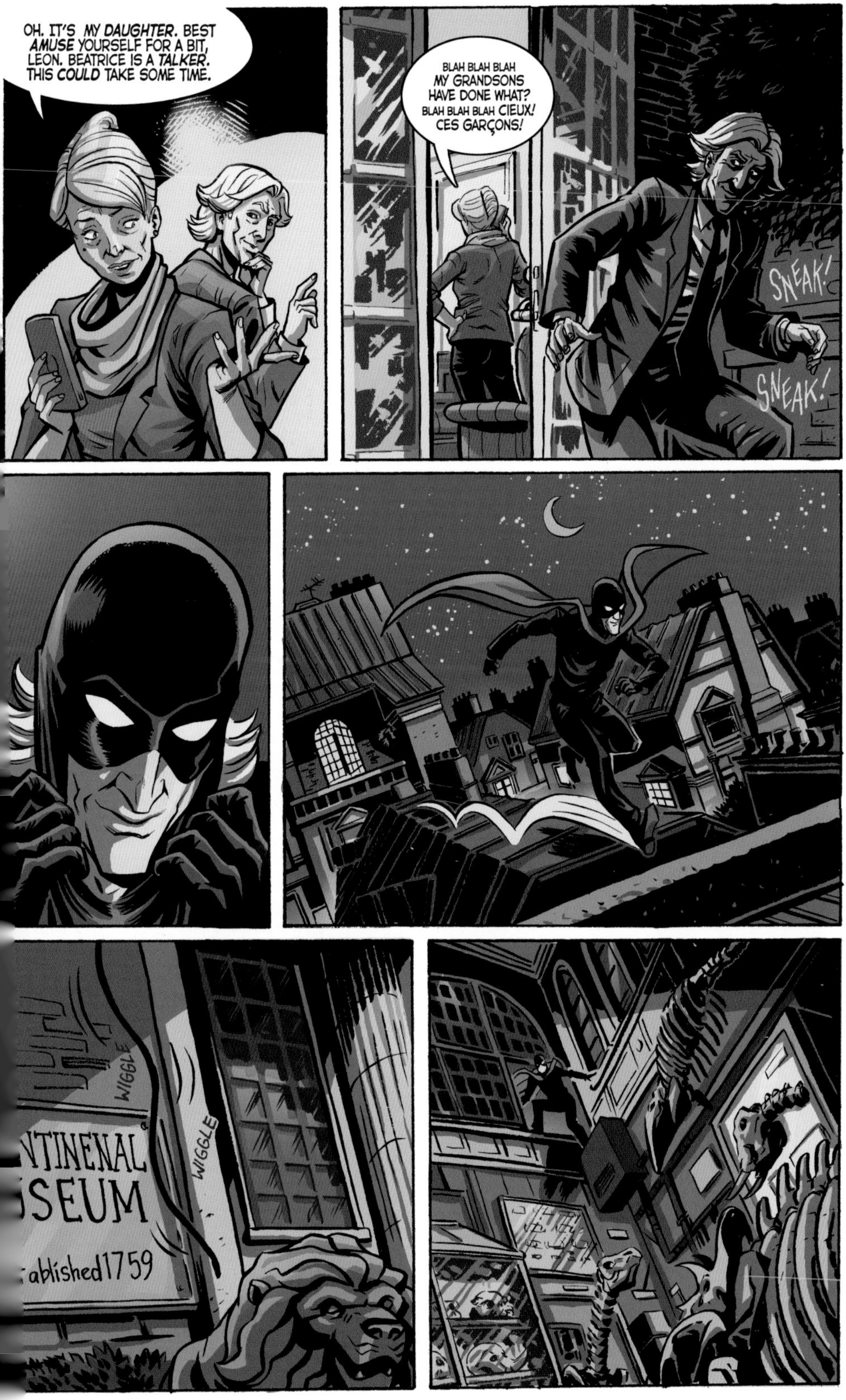
OH. IT'S MY DAUGHTER. BEST AMUSE YOURSELF FOR A BIT, LEON. BEATRICE IS A TALKER. THIS COULD TAKE SOME TIME.
BLAH BLAH BLAH MY GRANDSONS HAVE DONE WHAT? BLAH BLAH BLAH CIEUX! CES GARÇONS!
SNEAK!
SNEAK!
WIGGLE
WIGGLE
NTINENAL
SEUM
ablished1759

AND SOON...

AHH, THERE YOU ARE, LEON. SORRY TO TAKE SO LONG. BEATRICE WOULDN'T *STOP* CHATTING.

YOU WOULDN'T *BELIEVE* WHAT MISCHIEF MY GRANDCHILDREN GET INTO!

IT'S AS IF...OH. *OH! LOOK!* MY *GLASSES!* HERE THEY ARE! I MUST NOT HAVE *FORGOTTEN* THEM AFTER ALL!

SHALL WE CONTINUE OUR *READING*, THEN?

YES. PLEASE, LILLI, I'D LIKE THAT *VERY* MUCH.

THE END

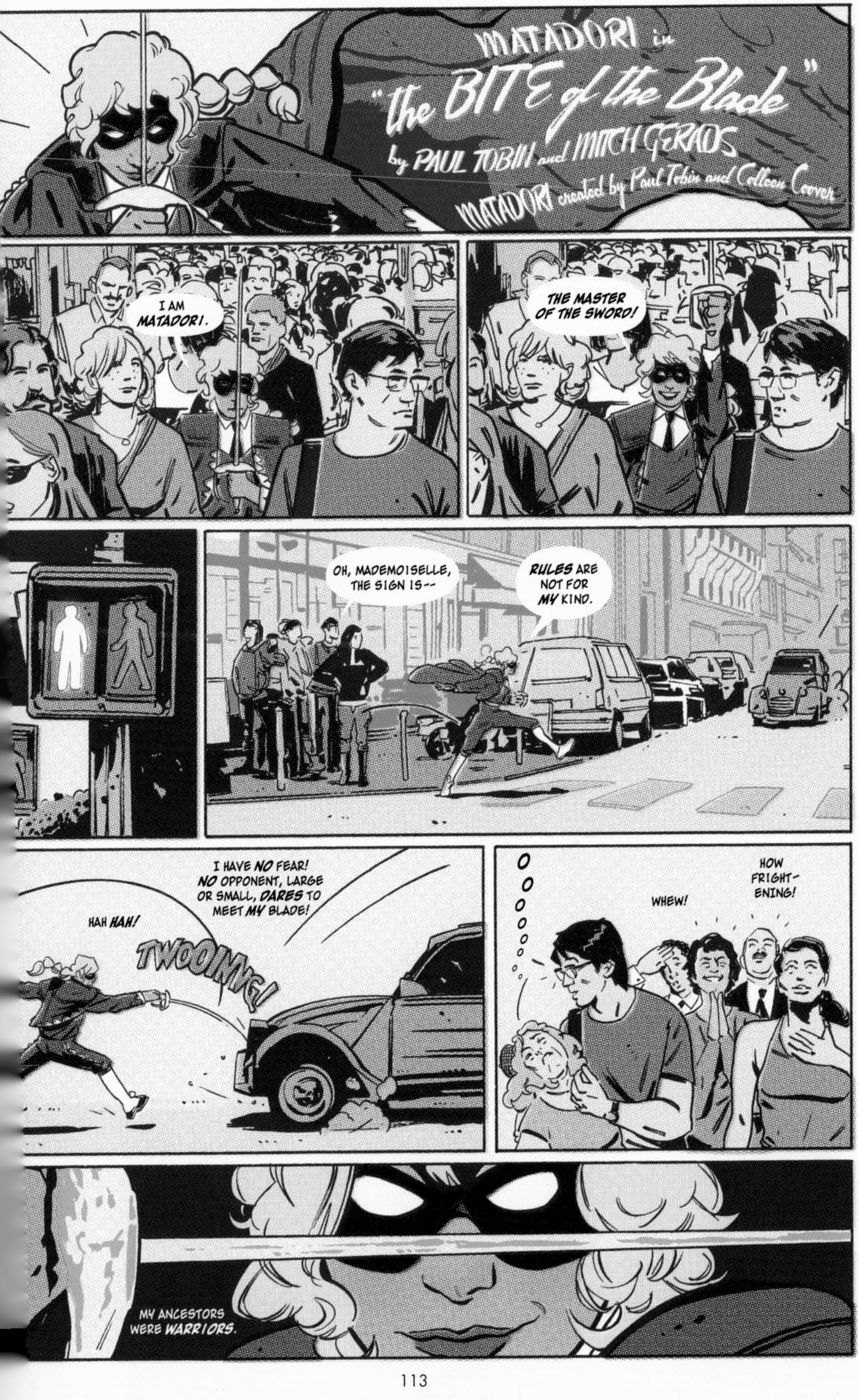
MATADORI in
"the BITE of the Blade"
by PAUL TOBIN and MITCH GERADS
MATADORI created by Paul Tobin and Colleen Coover
I AM MATADORI.
THE MASTER OF THE SWORD!
OH, MADEMOISELLE, THE SIGN IS--
RULES ARE NOT FOR MY KIND.
I HAVE NO FEAR! NO OPPONENT, LARGE OR SMALL, DARES TO MEET MY BLADE!
HAH HAH!
TWOOINNG!
WHEW!
HOW FRIGHT-ENING!
MY ANCESTORS WERE WARRIORS.

MY ANCESTORS WERE ASSASSINS.

EXPERTS WITH THE BLADE.

THE *BRUTALITY* OF A *BROADSWORD*.

THE *INTRIGUE* OF A *STILETTO*.

THE *FINESSE* OF A *RAPIER*.

I AM *MATADORI*.

I AM *UNMATCHED*.

THE GROUND *HEARS NOT* MY SILENT FOOTFALL, BUT *TREMBLES* JUST THE SAME. FOR *I* AM THE *DEADLIEST* OF ALL.

I AM *MATADORI*. I AM...

OOOO! CANDY!

SWOOOOSH!

114

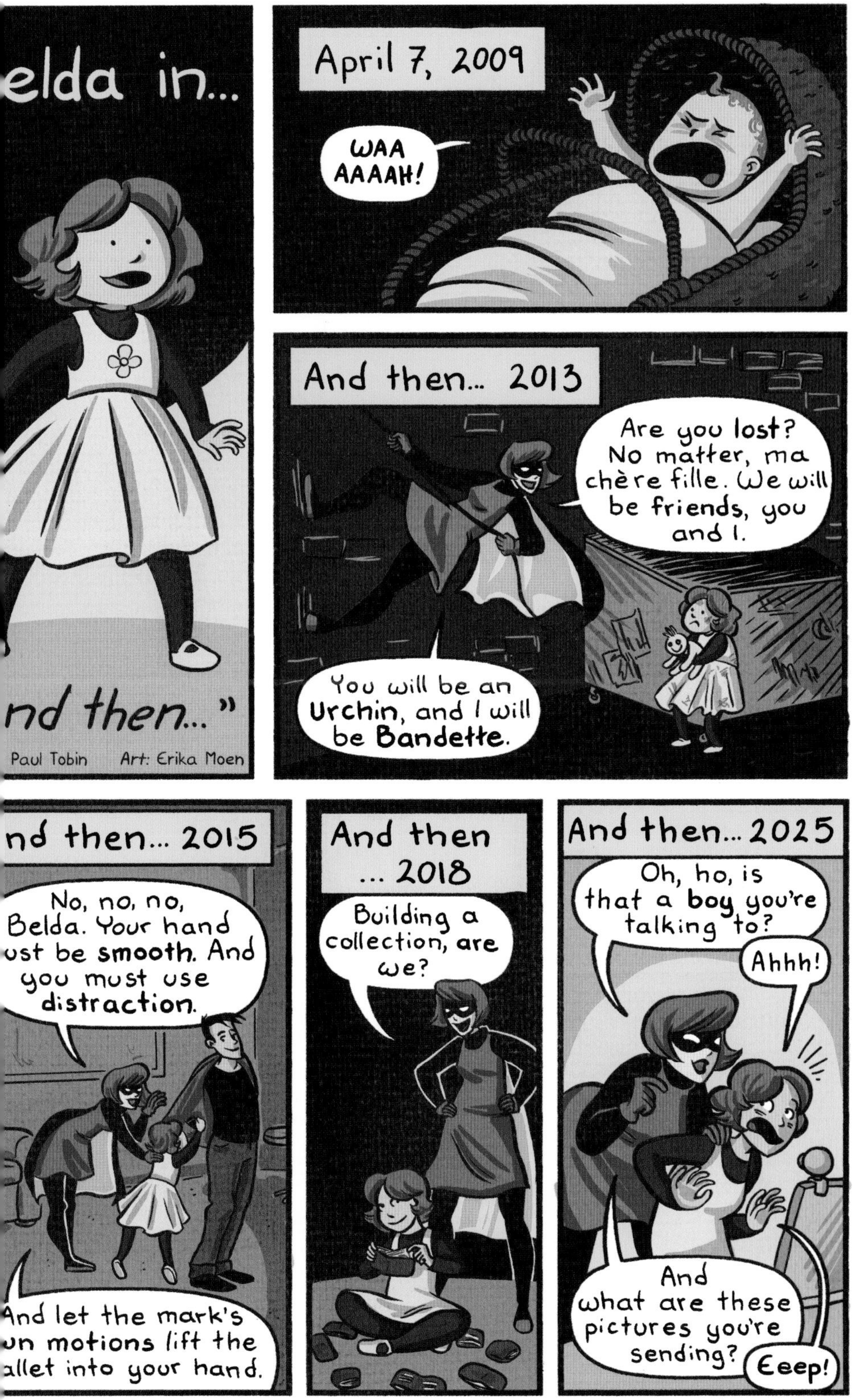

elda in...
nd then..."
Paul Tobin Art: Erika Moen
April 7, 2009
WAA AAAAH!
And then... 2013
Are you lost? No matter, ma chère fille. We will be friends, you and I.
You will be an Urchin, and I will be Bandette.
nd then... 2015
No, no, no, Belda. Your hand ust be smooth. And you must use distraction.
And let the mark's un motions lift the allet into your hand.
And then ... 2018
Building a collection, are we?
And then... 2025
Oh, ho, is that a boy you're talking to?
Ahhh!
And what are these pictures you're sending?
Eeep!

And then... 2030

Oh you silly criminals. Whatever do you think you're doing? Don't you know that...

...Ms. Midnight is here!

And then... 2050

And then... 2060

And then... 2107

I'm afraid there's nothing we can do. It's just... her time.

Can I see her?

Of course. She's just...

BELDA

Why... she's **gone!** But where...?

Hah! I'd bet we'll never know. I should have suspected as much.

Oh Belda. My Belda.

I'll miss you.

And then...?

The end.

Daniel's Story

By Paul Tobin

Illustrations by Colleen Coover

Bandette was absolutely breathtaking.

And utterly breathless.

She's often that way. It was three thirty-four in the morning. The moon and several cats were playing witness to Bandette's mischief. As always, they approved. She and I were on my motorbike. I was frantically driving, and she was mostly hugging me from behind, laughing in my ear, but occasionally standing up on the seat, facing backwards, taunting our pursuers while holding onto nothing but my hair, which I admit was uncomfortable. She had a small pouch containing an assortment of her mysterious thieving supplies, and more importantly a protected pocket in which was now nestled an oil painting of roughly fifty centimeters square. It depicted a naked woman smelling a

red flower and had been painted by Suzanne Valadon, who was not only one of Bandette's favorite painters but had also been a model for such luminaries as Renoir and Toulouse-Lautrec.

We had no time to admire the painting.

Bandette and I were carrying along at my motorbike's highest speed, which is unfortunately only fifty-three kilometers per hour . . . bouncing and skidding along on a cobblestone street and flashing past a mansion where Napoleon had not only once slept but . . . according to what Bandette whispered in my ear . . . had even had an affair with a chambermaid.

"Oh ho," she said. "What a thrill!"

"The liaison?" I asked.

"That too, Daniel. Oh, that naughty little emperor! Although he wasn't little. That's a myth, you know." She was standing again, this time facing forward with one foot on the rear of my motorbike's seat and the other on my shoulder. I've no idea how she could maintain her balance. Just looking at her makes me dizzy. Her laughter, her smile, everything makes me so dizzy. I could see her reflection in the shop windows as we charged past. Bandette was making a series of rude gestures to the five men in the black car that was less than a half block behind. Her cape was flapping so hard that I almost couldn't hear the bullets that were whizzing past us.

Almost.

· · · · · · · · · · · · ·

I have a small apartment in the corner of a famous clock tower. I suppose you could say I'm squatting there. It's rather makeshift. It consists of one room and a bath that is walled off only by a standing Japanese screen that Bandette "acquired" for me from the Louvre, one that depicts several scantily clad geisha waving at three samurai who are letting their horses drink from a stream. It had been in the museum's basements. Bandette claimed the Louvre would never display the piece[1], so it wasn't actually theft. I believe that's rather speculative reasoning, but I admit I like the screen. My bathtub is from the fifteenth century and has dragon's feet carved from

jade. It was also a gift from Bandette. Likewise my bed, a bed in which Madame de Pompadour once spent an evening. I built all four of my bookcases myself, but they are filled with Bandette's gifts. She's like a cat, always bringing mice to my door, though of course instead of rodents it's such things as *The Life of Gargantua and of Pantagruel*, a spirited and somewhat vulgar book by François Rabelais, first published during the sixteenth century in a series of five volumes. I was initially surprised she hadn't stolen me the original editions, but she'd wanted me to have the later printings with the illustrations by Gustave Doré. My

Bandette was making a series of rude gestures to the five men in the black car.

[1] She said, "But, Daniel, the geisha wear no tops! Their treasures are in view! What of the children who toddle through the Louvre? It would be scandalous to display such an item!" She was reasoning with me while holding the screen, perched outside my window. I argued that she loves scandal, which she admitted, but she somehow won our argument regardless, which came as no surprise. After the screen had been moved into my room, after Bandette was gone, I peered outside for where she could possibly have been standing. There was only the tiniest ledge. Barely two inches wide. I do not know how she does such things!

copy was autographed by Doré himself, along with a further, original illustration. It rests on a shelf next to another gift from Bandette, one of her very favorite books . . . *In Praise of Folly*, also from the sixteenth century. This book, in actuality more of a pamphlet, truly *is* the first edition[2]. Bandette told me that I was far too dear for any secondary copy. It was one of the first times we'd ever met. I'd been delivering an order of Massaman curry to what turned out to be an empty apartment. Empty, that is, except for the world's greatest thief. I'd knocked on the door. It had opened. It was Bandette. She took the curry, gave me enough money to cover the check five times over, and then handed me the book. The door closed. We hadn't spoken. I immediately opened the door. Bandette was gone. I was all the way outside and riding on my motorbike before I remembered that it is important to breathe.

Other gifts abound in my room. I suppose I have a fortune at hand, though of course I would never part with a single object. They are from the woman that I . . . well, I care more for her than for anyone else. For anything else. I could go on. But then I would feel like one of those poor fellows in Montmartre, writing their sentimental poetry while sipping coffee at over-priced cafés. That said, there is one monolithic difference between myself and those men. They are only writing about women.

, on the other hand, am speaking of a thief.

'm speaking of Bandette.

· · · · · · · · · · · · · · · · · · · ·

hree hours ago, my phone rang. The caller was listed as *unknown*. This is not uncommon. answered. It was Bandette.

"You are speaking to Bandette!" she said. She sounded jealous of my luck.

"Hello!" I said. My voice squeaked. This is something else that is not uncommon. My skin shivers when I hear her voice or see her face. My heart thumps. My words fail. Everything but my nerve quivers. Strangely, my nerve is fine. She makes me feel reckless.

"Do you feel reckless, Daniel?" she asked on the phone. Ahh, see there? It's not uncommon for her to pluck thoughts from my mind! It is somewhat unsettling. But I suppose an uncommon woman does uncommon things.

"Reckless?" I asked.

"Yes! I have found great dangers! We should explore them! Quickly! What if they make an escape?"

"An escape?"

"Are you dressed?"

"What? Mostly."

"You'll need a sweater. The night is chilly. We will be traveling at high speeds."

"That sounds . . ."

"Bring your scooter, yes?"

"Yes. But I thought you said we'd be traveling at high speeds?" I was trying to put on a sweater with one hand while talking on the phone with the other, all the while searching for my keys.

"You jest, Daniel. These amusements of yours are one reason why Bandette calls you. You

he author is Desiderius Erasmus Roterodamus. The character of Folly had *Plutus* and *Freshness* as her parents, meaning a god of wealth
nd a nymph. Among her companions are *Kolakia* (flattery) and *Hedone* (pleasure) and *Anoia* . . . madness. Folly often states that any
e without her would be lifeless and dull, that "you'll find nothing frolic or fortunate that it owes not to me." I can't read the book. It's in
tin. Bandette has to read it to me, which she loves to do as long as I keep giving her candy bars.

have the fox's wits. Do you much mind being shot at?"

"Is this a trick question?"

"All questions are tricks, Daniel. Didn't you know? I am sending you a map. Could I bother you to pick me up? I'll be in the chestnut tree on the corner. Several men are searching below, rudely intending to shoot me. Make haste! Oh . . . and bring candy bars!"

The call ended. A map appeared on my display. A glowing dot. Twenty-seven blocks away.

I tugged my sweater into place.

I sighed.

But I smiled.

There was work to do.

. . . .

It wasn't difficult to find the tree. It was a large chestnut in full roaring bloom, meaning that all of its branches and, presumably, the greatest of all thieves were hidden in the great depths of the leaves. There were five men gathered on the sidewalk below. When I first turned the corner onto the street they were carrying guns, but they hid them as I neared. One of the men was trying to climb the tree. They'd pulled a car onto the sidewalk and parked it up against the tree, and he was standing on the roof, struggling to reach the lower branches. I drove past, gauging the state of affairs.

My phone rang. It was Bandette. "You have driven past me," she said.

"Yes. Because . . ."

"Do it again. But, faster, Daniel. Much faster."

"Oh. Okay."

When I reached the end of the block I turned my motorbike around. The men were starting to take notice of me. Nothing to do about that. I looked behind me to make sure my delivery satchels . . . the ones where I normally carry food for my Rad Thai delivery job but which were currently full of candy bars . . . were secure. I rubbed the good luck charm that dangles from my crossbars[3] and then, with a deep breath, I twisted the throttle. Instantly, I was whooshing down the street at speeds approaching, well, thirty kilometers per hour.

So, no, not very fast.

I was fifty yards from the men. My speedometer was now showing forty. The men were no longer doing a very good job of hiding their guns. They weren't pointing them at me, though, so why complain?

I was twenty yards away. One of the men was indeed now pointing his gun roughly in my direction, but I doubted the wisdom of registering any complaint.

I was ten yards away when I heard the shout from the center of the tree. It was Bandette's voice. At amazing volume. The men jumped in startled fright and stared up at the tree. But by then it was too late.

There she was.

She burst out of the center of the tree as if she was a bird in flight. The leaves of the tree

[3] It's five centimeters tall. The vague shape of a chubby woman. Bandette tells me she found it in "some president's house." That's all she will say. When I ask for more she just laughs. Infuriating. I've even offered her an entire box of Chocoboliks, her favorite candy bar, if she'll tell, but she only smiles.

120

seemed to part for her out of respect. Her leap was beyond the abilities of any Olympic athlete. Her smile was Bandette's. There is no other measurement.

Her smile was Bandette's.

The arc of her leap took her far out into the street. I maintained my speed. Stayed on course. Steadied my nerve. When she landed on the back of my motorbike there wasn't near the impact I might have expected. Gravity rarely chastises Bandette for her actions. They are far too good of friends.

. . . .

The first time I met Bandette I was at Oubliette, meaning that bookseller you can find along the Seine, should you be in Paris. Look for the red sign with the book and the mouse. The stacks at the front of the store are filled with the latest romances and thrillers, but the rear of the store specializes, thanks to M. Harnois, in books of great age and rarity.[4] I'd been working a summer job, helping a friend with a tour group. The tourists were allowed to touch a priceless original copy of Swift's *A Modest Proposal*, although it was held in a protective sleeve. I had it in my hands when it happened.

A noise from the rafters.

I looked up.

A blur of red and yellow.

Then it was gone.

Did any of you see that?" I asked. The tour group, as one, shook their heads. They'd seen nothing. They'd traveled to Paris to look, but

. . . hadn't. I stared up to the rafters, but the shelves nearly reached them, and the lights were hung on cords, and there was much darkness. I could see nothing.

"Do we get to hold it?" an elderly woman asked me, gesturing to the book in my hands. Her name was Edith. She was wearing a red box hat with several blue flowers pinned to its side. She had a thousand lines on her face and also a constant smile and she had been flirting with me in shameless fashion. I'd been flirting back. Why not? That is Paris.

"Of course," I'd said, handing her the book. The woman wore white gloves and her fingers trembled when she touched the treasure. The small crowd gathered around her, respectfully, if impatiently, waiting their turn. There were expressions of interest in French, German, Dutch, and English. One Arabic couple was asking me how many other copies of the book might still exist when a candy bar wrapper fell from the rafters and landed on Edith's box hat. It was a Chocobolik wrapper, meaning that dark candy bar with the almonds and the single line of peanut butter crossing the bar in a diagonal fashion. The wrapper is dark black. It clashed with the red hat and its decorative blue flowers. Nobody else noticed, not even

A candy bar wrapper fell from the rafters and landed on Edith's box hat.

Eugène Harnois is the ageless proprietor of Oubliette. He seems to have reached the age of eighty and then entirely ceased aging. This may have happened a year ago. Or several decades in the past. Eugène no longer runs the day-to-day operations of the store, preferring to hire students from the École Polytechnique in order to add charm to the lives of these burgeoning scientists.

Edith, intent as they were upon the Swift book. I reached out and plucked the wrapper from Edith's hat. She gave me an odd look.

"Only touching the flowers to see if they're real," I told her. "I love flowers." She blushed and handed *A Modest Proposal* to another, taking me by my arm and asking me endless questions. The tour continued. We saw several other treasures, and M. Harnois spoke to my group on the topic of early publications and printing presses. He was speaking of scriptoriums, meaning the monastic workshops where books were copied or restored, when it happened.

"Pssssst," I heard. It came from a shelf next to me. I looked, but no one was there. I returned my gaze to the tour group, and M. Harnois.

"I am saying '*psssst*' to you!" came a voice. It was Bandette's voice. For those of you unlucky enough to have never heard her, she is music. Reckless music, like a gypsy's song. Her voice bubbles. Leaps. It has a low throaty quality, or a high and impish tone. The woman's voice is a hundred different songs. It had me in an instant. Just her voice and I was lured.

Unfortunately I was only lured to gaze at a selection of early twentieth century romances lined up along a shelf. There was nothing else to be seen.

"Move some books out of the way, Daniel," she said. I did, sliding aside a stack of American pulp magazines with such titles as *Rangeland Romance*, *Golden West*, and *Lariat*.

And then . . .

smiling at me from the other side of the bookcase . . .

there she was . . .

Bandette.

And my life changed.

"How did you know my name?" I asked. It was the first question I ever asked her. It would not be the last. Bandette is a woman of mystery. Enigmas spill away from her like sparkles from a ruby.

"Because I have stolen your wallet," she said, as if my question was obvious and absurd. She pushed my wallet through the gap in the bookshelf.

"How?" I asked.

"With thievery," she answered. "The greatest of arts. You are in the presence of a master. Have you heard of Bandette?"

"You stole my wallet?" I was putting it back in my pocket. "Really? I can't believe it!"

She frowned, but she did so in that way that she does, where the frown is like a drum roll for a smile. For the briefest of instants, she disappeared. I barely had time to blink.

Then she passed my wallet through the bookcase to me.

"I have done it again," she said. "Does this help your belief? You must have faith in thievery, *Daniel-who-flirts-with-elderly-women*!"

I looked down to the bookcase. There was a gap in a lower shelf, waist height. Is that how she had . . . ?

I looked back up and she was gone. My heart felt, well . . . I am trying to avoid any poetry. Let me simply say that it felt like my heart was angry with me. It was calling me a fool.

Bandette was gone.

I worried that I would never see her again.

And then . . . smiling at me from the other side of the bookcase . . .
there she was . . . Bandette.

Also my coffee. Grabbing for the falling water, I accidentally flung the remainder of my crêpe onto the sidewalk.

"I'm a fool!" I blurted, aghast at my clumsiness in the presence of such grace.

"Yes, that is true, Daniel," Bandette said. "But that took me only moments to decide. My thoughts were somewhere else. I have been thinking we should be friends." She was mopping up my spills with one hand, holding out her other for me to shake.

"Friends?" I said, as if I were an imbecile with no idea of the word's meaning. To be fair, at the time, I had little grasp on the meaning of anything. I felt as if I were suddenly walking a high wire.

- - - - - - - - - - - - - - - - - - -

t was twenty minutes later when she sat down next to me at a sidewalk café. Possibly you know the café, Imp's Boudoir, where they serve the dessert crêpes. They mix fruit jams with cheeses and they become quite a treat. Unfortunately, I could barely taste mine, a raspberry and asiago combination. It tasted like dirt. It tasted like sorrow. It tasted like I would never again see the mysterious and alluring figure who . . .

Bandette has been thinking," she said. She was seated across from me. I had no idea how long she had been there. I spilled my water.

"Exactly," Bandette said. "Friends!" She sat. Crossed her legs. Waved for the waiter's attentions. "We're agreed, then. How marvelous. How much in your life have you stolen, and from whom?"

"Stolen?"

"Nothing, then? Do you like croissants? Capes? Fan dancers? Oscar Wilde and Vincent van Gogh?"

"I suppose. Yes. All of them."

She stared at me through a water carafe that she'd picked up from the table. It distorted her face so that the black mask seemed to wrap around the entirety of the carafe, with her stern expression magnified many times over.

Bandette said, "Daniel, do not *suppose*. If you stand on a ledge, you cannot merely *suppose* you will not fall. You must entirely believe in yourself and in your ability. Only then will you not be *chastised*." She put down the carafe and said, "Now then, we will try again. Do you like croissants?"

"Absolutely. They are delicious."

"Ballerinas?"

"Of course. Beyond question."

"Brass doorknobs and pen quills?"

"I find them romantic."

"Do you like Bandette?" she said. She dipped her fingers in the carafe and flicked a spray of water onto my face. I blinked. My mouth would not open. I was incapable of uttering a single sound. She laughed. It echoed all through the streets.

"You're keeping words that are meant for me," Bandette said. She made a moue and tapped a finger on my cheek. "And you claim you've never stolen anything!"

· · · · · · · · · · · · · · · · · · · ·

Twenty minutes later, I could not remember a time when Bandette had not been my friend. She'd paid our café check with money extracted from a selection of wallets in her purse. We sat atop Notre Dame and she read to me from a book she'd produced from a pocket in her cape's interior, unwrapping the book from within what seemed to be butcher's paper. It was an original 1897 hardback edition of *The Invisible Man* by H. G. Wells. Bandette stood on the edge of a precipice, her red gloves nearly matching the color of the binding, somehow keeping her smile in place even while she was reading, with her voice booming out over the square, *"The stranger came early in February, one wintry day, through a biting wind and a driving snow, the last snowfall of the year, over the down, walking from Bramblehurst railway station, and carrying a little black portmanteau in his thickly gloved hand."*

· · · · · · · · · · · · · · · · · · · ·

"Thank you for picking me up, dear Daniel," Bandette said, momentarily snuggling behind me on my scooter. I could feel the stolen Valadon painting she had tucked up into her cape. From where she might have stolen it, I would probably never know. She prefers to remain secretive. I *do* know that, *whoever* she had stolen it from, they were *mad*. The men in the car refused to give up. Would they never run out of bullets? They were everywhere! I kept as low as possible and urged Bandette to do the same, but she only laughed, ruffled my hair, and then clamped her hands over my eyes. I immediately began swerving all over the street, careening along for several blocks as she called out, "Right! Left! Oh, Daniel, that charming store is having a special sale on éclairs! If only we had time to stop!" She sounded so wistful. As for myself, I believe I was screaming.

"My eyes!" I yelled. "Uncover my eyes!"

"Oh no no *no*! That I will *not* do! You would not wish to see where we are about to go. It would unsettle you, my friend."

I said, "What do . . . ?" but at that moment the street fell away from my motorbike. We were airborne. Or rather we were falling. Bandette has often told me that falling is the same as being airborne but that is most decidedly not true.

Her gloved hands left my eyes, allowing me to see. I gulped and looked to see where tell me some fabulous method of avoiding our onrushing fate.

"Turn off your headlamp, Daniel," she whispered. "And the engine, too." It wasn't what I wanted to hear. This wasn't salvation . . . it only meant that the gunmen would arrive to find us sodden in the canal, my scooter descending into the depths, and the only change would be that we wouldn't . . .

"*PFWEEEEEET!*"

Bandette blew a whistle. It was quite close to my ear, and I was momentarily stunned, so that it was all I could do to follow her instructions, turning the key on my motorbike, killing the engine, and dousing the headlamp just as a net shot out from under the bridge, capturing me, capturing my motorbike, and capturing . . .

. . . where was Bandette?

The gunmen's car had screeched to a halt at the edge of the canal. They were yelling in German, scouring the surrounding area.

Bandette had taken us.

It chanced that we had been going over the Passerelle Bichat, the bridge over the Canal Saint-Martin. Somehow we'd gone off the side and were now plummeting for the water. I saw no possible way to avoid crashing into the canal. Worse, I could hear the squealing roar of the black car rounding the corner. They would soon arrive and would undoubtedly find Bandette and me treading water, with my motorbike sinking below us, the headlamp shining up from the depths, illuminating us from below so that the gunmen would have an easier time with the targeting.

Bandette's mouth moved close to my ear. My heart sung at this. She was obviously about to

It was five of my fellow urchins who had caught me in the net. It was Tommy. It was Freckles. And it was the Three Ballerinas, meaning Kiyomi, Adalind, and Manon. They were hanging from the bottom of the bridge, all of them with mountain-climbing equipment, and only Kiyomi let out the smallest of noises and a whisper of "*pardonnez-moi!*" with the effort of reeling in the net and securing both my scooter and myself out of sight beneath the bridge.

But where was Bandette?

"Where . . ." I said, but Adalind held up a finger to my lips. She leaned in so close that her hair was brushing my cheeks through the netting. She said, "Bandette will be back *tout de suite*, but she has mentioned you brought candy bars, no?"

"Yes," I said. "They're in my delivery satchels, but where . . ." Manon's finger came out to rest on my lips along with Adalind's, which was still in place. It was all I could do to not struggle, but the movement would have given our position away. The gunmen's car had screeched to a halt at the edge of the canal. They were yelling in German, scouring the surrounding area. I was trapped in the net beneath the bridge, but . . . where was Bandette?

"The candy bars are here!" Freckles whispered. They began opening the wrappers, the noises of this mingling with that of the water running below us, lost to the gunmen's ears.

"The whistle was our signal," Tommy whispered. "Do you want a candy bar?"

"I want Bandette!" I hissed, careful to keep my voice low. Tommy laughed at this. Freckles had the slightest of giggles. All three of the ballerinas clucked their tongues. I started to tell them I'd meant that I wanted to know where Bandette *was*, not that I wanted Bandette as a girlfriend or anything silly like that, that they'd misunderstood what I meant to say, but Manon's finger reached out to stop my lips once again.

"Let truth keep its voice," she said. Instead of further complicating the misunderstanding, I only nodded. What else could I do? I had to remain silent, and motionless. One of the gunmen was now peering beneath the bridge, searching for us, but we were luckily lost in the darkness. They would not see us. There was no problem.

Except . . .

He had a flashlight.

The beam came on. It flashed beneath the bridge. And then up to us. He let out a grunt at

"I attack with cucumbers!" Bandette yelled out.

what he was seeing.

"Hello!" Adalind said to him. "Let this be a secret, yes?"

"Over here!" he yelled out to the others, pointing his gun at us.

"Oh, you rascal!" Adalind said. "No candy bars for you!" I was struggling to get free of the net. If only I could drop to the ground, perhaps I could overpower him. I couldn't let the others be in danger. To be an urchin is to protect one another, and if we . . .

A cucumber hit the man in the head. It dazed him. The flashlight fell from his hands, but he retained his grip on the gun.

"I attack with cucumbers!" Bandette yelled out. A volley of three more of them came from a rooftop. They hit the man in his chest and head, staggering him.

"More cucumbers!" Bandette shouted from the darkness. "This is quite fearsome!" Only a moment later she dropped down to the stree rolling with impact and then springing u onto the man's shoulders. Then, latching he legs around his neck, she flipped backward

126

landing just on the edge of the canal.

The gunman fell into the water.

"Presto!" Bandette laughed. "The pool is now open!" It was at that moment that the other gunmen came running. They began firing at Bandette, the only one of us they could see. Bullets began to rain down on the cobblestones around her.

"Bullets!" she said. "How frightening! Daniel, a candy bar if you would!" I wormed an arm free and tossed her a Chocobolik. She caught it without looking and hurriedly freed it from its wrapper. She chomped off a large bite. The bullets were all around her. Missing her by inches. I was shivering with fear and clawing at the net that held me. Suddenly, Bandette cried out.

"**OH!**" she gasped. "This candy is so delicious!" She chewed and chewed, and then she swallowed and brought a whistle to her lips.

"**PFWEEEEEET!**" The whistle rang out.

"The second signal!" Tommy said. I lo oked back to the urchins. Kiyomi was holding a small remote control. She touched a button.

And the night came alive with fireworks.

They erupted from the sides of the canal. From beneath the bridge. From the rooftops of nearby buildings and even from the walkway beneath the feet of the gunmen. It blinded them. Disoriented them. They stumbled and staggered into the canal, splashing within, joining the first man in the waters. In moments I was free of the netting and standing with Bandette. The others soon joined me. The gunmen were floundering helpless in the waters as the other urchins ran off. Bandette and I leapt onto my motorbike and we soared away down the street, with her holding tight and laughing behind me. The fireworks were still exploding all around.

"You set this up?" I said, gesturing to the fireworks, to all of the explosions of red, blue, orange, and yellow . . . to these and all the other colors soaring vibrantly about in the sky, falling to the streets all around us.

"True," she acknowledged. "I have indeed done this!" She snuggled closer.

"And all to make your escape when the time came?"

"*Non*, Daniel!" she said, aghast. "I could have *stolen* an escape at any time! Am I not the master thief?"

I nodded that she was. That *of course* she was.

"Then why?" I asked.

"Because it is beautiful," Bandette said, speaking as if I were a fool.

And of course I have been.

Always.

Since the day I first met her. ❖

The night came alive with fireworks.

WHAT'S BANDETTE STOLEN *NOW?*

Here we take a quick look at some of the many objects that Bandette has liberated from their owners, and speak a bit about why the teenaged master thief would do such a thing, beyond the fact that it is daring and thrilling to purloin a few treasures, lending someone a stimulating sense of audacious accomplishment that entirely dwarfs the worth of the masterpieces themselves! But it's wrong to steal, of course. Entirely wrong.

Here, Bandette steals several miniature Rembrandt illustrations. Rembrandt van Rijn (1606–1669) is one of *the* giants, and because of this people tend to think of his works on a grand scale, but in actuality a great many of his surviving works are tiny in size, no larger than baseball cards, though still quite beautiful in their detail.

A Rembrandt self-portrait with a bounty of detail and expression, all in a pint-sized package. I like to think this is one of the illustrations that Bandette purloined, and that it now rests in a cameo frame on her dresser, next to several Chocobolik candy wrappers and a collection of vintage skeleton keys.

A black crayon drawing. I love how Rembran captured the leathery skin. This is another on that Bandette stole. I'm just sure of it.

Bandette is not the only master thief in our world. Here, Monsieur is in the process of stealing the 1794 Flowing Hair Silver Dollar.

Often named as the world's most expensive coin. Only some 130 of these coins are known to exist, and examples have sold for as much as ten million dollars.

These vintage bottles of absinthe are still on Bandette's "to steal" list at press time! Who doesn't like a classic bottle of wine, or . . . absinthe? C. Comoz opened his deliciously inebriating company in 1870, in France's Savoie region, basing his "Absinthe des Alpes" on a local recipe incorporating mountain herbs.

The example seen here is from 1870, as no known intact bottles of 1871 vintage exist. We can also see the art for the labels. Amazingly, it is the leader of FINIS, Absinthe himself, who is rumored to possess seventy-two bottles (!) of the 1871 vintage, having foully murdered to obtain them. Certainly either Bandette or Monsieur will use a bit more panache, craft, and whimsy, should they somehow uncover the hiding place of these vintage bottles.

Jane Avril (1868–1943) was the high-stepping French cancan dancer who was one of Toulouse-Lautrec's favorite subjects to illustrate. He often used her to advertise the legendary Moulin Rouge, where Jane was a headline performer.

Walking through one of Bandette's many secret lairs, a treasure is revealed on the wall. An original work by Henri de Toulouse-Lautrec, one depicting Jane Avril.

Another treasure seen on a hideout's wall, a vintage poster of a performing magician. Bandette's collection of vintage posters is quite extensive, encompassing magicians, circuses, and various other celebrities of the performing arts. But . . . who is Madame Presto, and does she have any connection to the world's most famous and talented thief?

The posters of Miss Baldwin (circa 1890) are some of Bandette's favorites.

WRITING Bandette

These pages contain an excerpt from Paul's script for *Bandette* #1.

Page One (5 Panels)

PANEL 1: At a rich French mansion in the middle of the city, but focused on a brick fence that separates the lawn from the sidewalk. Very close in on this fence, and on several birds (starlings?) perched on the wall. It's midday.

PANEL 2: Boom! Bandette pops up into view. Just head and shoulders as she begins to pull herself up and over the wall. She's super happy. Think *Amélie* cute. The birds are scattering.

> BANDETTE: **Presto!**

PANEL 3: Bandette now creeeeeeping across the small lawn. She's going past two slumbering guard dogs, who do not notice her. Bandette making the *shhhhh* gesture with a finger to her mouth. This mansion is in the middle of the city . . . so the lawn is small.

> BANDETTE: Keep **sleeping**, doggies. Keep sleeping **deep**. Keep **sleeping**, doggies. Or else I will **weep**.

> LETTERING NOTE: *Give Bandette's words "music" to them, as if she is singing.*

PANEL 4: Bandette has crawled up a wall and is going in through a 2nd story window.

> BANDETTE: **Hark**! What **thief** through yonder window **breaks**?

PANEL 5: Bandette now creeping down a hallway. This place is NICE!

Page Two (5 Panels)

PANEL 1: Bandette has run across another dog, this one just in the hallway. It's a small dog, cute. Bandette has her hands on knees, looking down at the dog in the *"OMG, aren't you the CUTEST!"* pose. The dog is happy to see her.

> BANDETTE: **Ooh**! Another **doggie**.

> BANDETTE (2nd balloon): Hello, cutie. My name is **Bandette**. Want to come along with me on a **robbery**?

> DOG: **Ruff!**

PANEL 2: Bandette walking off down the hall, looking fondly back over her shoulder to the dog, which is following her.

> BANDETTE: **Really**? You **do**?

> BANDETTE (2nd balloon): Oh, **naughty dog!** You're as bad as a **cat!**

PANEL 3: Bandette picking the lock of a doorway, very happily talking to the dog as she does.

> BANDETTE: Your master has several drawings by **Rembrandt**. **Very** tiny. But . . . **wow**. The **line work!** The **expressions!**

> BANDETTE (2nd balloon): You **DO** like Rembrandt, don't you?

> DOG: **Ruff!**

PANEL 4: Bandette going into a room that's FULL of art. We don't really need to see much of the room, yet . . . just that she is going in. She is carrying the dog, rubbing his head fondly, talking to him.

> BANDETTE: And how about your **master**? You like **him**? He's kind of a **bad guy**, you know. He sells weapons to some very shady **men**, underworld **organizations**, and nasty **governments**.

> BANDETTE (2nd balloon): He's a very **busy** bad man.

PANEL 5: Bandette and a wall of art. There is a small (ornate) table in front of the wall, where Bandette has placed the dog. She is taking some very small pieces of art off the wall . . . the Rembrandts . . . see below for example/reference.

> BANDETTE: And so . . . he is **thieved**.

> BANDETTE (2nd balloon): This is called **justice**. Or **robbery**. One of the two.

A Rembrandt example. Remy did lots of small drawings. This example is less than two inches high.

Page Three (5 Panels)

PANEL 1: Bandette showing the small Rembrandts (she has stolen four or five of them) to the dog, which is sniffing at them with curiosity.

> BANDETTE: Do you **like** them? Aren't they **wonderful**?

> BANDETTE (2nd balloon): Now, **don't** eat them. They are **NOT** biscuits.

PANEL 2: Bandette back out in the hall. Walking around, somewhat lost. The dog is trotting behind her. She's about to go through a door at the end of the hall, at an intersection.

> BANDETTE: Your master will be **quite** surprised to find them **missing** when he comes home from his trip. I **wish** I could see his **face!**

> BANDETTE (2nd balloon): Now, oh, **where** was the way out? Was it . . . over **here**?

PANEL 3: Interior view of the room she's coming into. Wide view of the whole room. It's a nice library area (or whatever) that's somewhat suitable for seductions, and a man is RIGHT HELL SEDUCING a girl on a couch (boxers & brassieres), but their love-making is being interrupted by Bandette, who has come in through the door and is looking at them, somewhat taken aback.

> BANDETTE: Oops.

PANEL 4: A moment later. Everyone looking at each other in confusion/surprise/embarrassment. Bandette giving a grimace and a tiny wave.

> BANDETTE: Oh. Hi.

PANEL 5: Bandette now SPEEDING out of the doorway and into the hall. She's still carrying the Rembrandts. Time to RUN!

> WORD BALLOON/YELL COMING FROM OPEN DOORWAY: **Guards!**

> BANDETTE: How **DARE** he! He was **NOT** supposed to be at home today!

Drawing Bandette

This section expands on the *Bandette* process posts from Colleen's blog.

PART ONE: DESIGN, DRAW, DONE

The technique I use to create the art of *Bandette* is one of those happy accidents that you rarely stumble upon. The result of experimentation with graphics programs and physical media that, when it all clicks into place, makes an artist like me do a little happy dance and want to tell the world all about it. So here it is: the secret instructions for creating the look of *Bandette*!

Components!

A computer
You may find it surprising in the course of this tutorial just how much I rely upon digital media to create the art of *Bandette*! I use a MacBook Pro.

A digital drawing table
I use a Wacom Cintiq 12WX. There are a lot of drawing tablets available, but I wouldn't want to buy any product that doesn't use Wacom tech. They're the best.

Manga Studio by Smith Micro Software
Manga Studio is a graphics utility that was developed specifically for use by comic book artists. I used Manga Studio EX4 during the creation of *Bandette* issues #1–#4 and the excellent new Manga Studio 5E while working on issue #5.

Photoshop by Adobe Systems
I use Photoshop primarily for color and lettering. Manga Studio has greatly improved its color application with version 5E, but so far Photoshop is easier and faster for me, so I'm sticking to it. I use Photoshop CS3. Not the most recent version, but it works for me!

A working knowledge of the above two programs
You're on your own there, I'm afraid, but I'll try not to make this too complicated.

A color printer
Must be capable of handling Bristol bond paper.

Bristol bond paper

For most comics art, the nicer and more expensive the paper, the better. But for *Bandette*, I have found that low-grade Bristol bond with a vellum, or slightly rough, texture works best.

Ink

I use Koh-I-Noor Rapidograph Ultradraw ink, which is formulated to be black, waterproof, and fast drying on the page. WARNING: be sure you get Rapidograph Ultradraw, *not* Universal or Rapidraw inks, for comics art! They will clog on your brush. Yuck!

Brush

Almost a standard in the comics industry, I use a Winsor & Newton Series 7 Watercolor Round, size 2. I can rattle off a request for one of these sable-hair brushes at any art supply store without pausing to think. They're a little pricey, and they're not always perfect, but in my experience they are the most reliable in quality and performance and worth the cost.

Assembly!

1. Rough layouts

In the Manga Studio program, I lay out the panels for the page and sketch in the action, usually using a big, fat pen setting so I won't be tempted to start drawing with too much detail. It doesn't look like much at this point—just a rough indication of where to place everything. (*fig. 1*)

figure 1

2. "Penciling"

In traditional comics art, the "pencils" are just that: a drawing in pencil, which is then retraced in ink to provide nice, crisp lines for print. The penciling stage is usually where most of the pretty rendering happens.

I do not pencil *Bandette* in the traditional manner. Instead, I create new layers in the same Manga Studio file where I roughed out the page design, and tighten up the layout with more precise tool settings. Essentially, I create digital "pencils." (*fig. 2*)

figure 2

3. Print the pencils

I convert the art to pale blue in Photoshop (*fig. 3*) and print it onto Bristol bond paper with a color printer.

figure 3

4. Ink the page

I use a technique of drawing called ink wash, which uses layers of watered-down ink to create gray tones. The blue lines of the printed "pencils" are still visible, and will run when they get wet, but that's okay! (*fig. 4*)

figure 4

Ink wash is a lot like using watercolor paint, though of course with only one hue (gray). Unlike watercolor paint, ink wash cannot be blended once it's on the page, so the artist has to be sure she has the mixture of ink and water she wants before she makes her brush strokes!

This is the only stage in my art process that uses physical media on paper, and it is my favorite.

5. Drop the blue lines

Things get a little technical here. I make a scan of the art in RGB color, and open the file in Photoshop. To drop the blue lines out, I go into Channels (Window –> Channels) and delete the green and cyan channels by dragging them into the little trashcan icon there.

This process flattens the image and converts its mode to Multichannel. The mode must be converted to grayscale (Image –> Mode) before I can move on. The art will be a little washed out at this point, so I adjust the levels (Image –> Adjust –> Levels) until the black areas are nice and dark, and the white areas are crispy white! (*fig. 5*)

figure 5

6. Letters and panel borders

I make panel borders with the Rectangular Marquee tool, leaving the space for the panels themselves "empty." Lettering can be done with a digital font, or by hand with the drawing tablet. I use a comics font for dialogue and create word balloons with the Elliptical Marquee tool, and I draw sound effects by hand. I use many layers for lettering, so that I can move each bit of text or graphics around independently. I group all these layers together so I can hide them while I move on to coloring. (Click off the little eye icon next to the layer group in the Layers window.) That group of layers is arranged above the art and color layers, and the panel border layer goes on top of everything else. (*fig. 6*)

figure 6

135

I use Photoshop for lettering; a lot of people prefer Adobe Illustrator. Your mileage may vary.

7. Colorize the ink layer

Once the lettering layers are hidden, the file has to be converted to RGB mode so that color can be applied (Image -> Mode). *NOTE: when you convert the file, Photoshop will ask if you'd like to flatten the image. Say no!*

I like to make the inks a nice, warm, sepia brown. It both gives the art a bit more life, and it blends with color in a pleasing way. I select the ink layer, and set a brown I have saved in my swatches as the foreground color, then use Hue & Saturation (Image -> Adjustments -> Hue & Saturation) and check the little box labeled Colorize. That's it! (*fig.7*)

figure 7

Finally, I change the Blend Mode of the ink layer from Normal to Multiply (Layer -> Layer Style -> Blending Options). This basically makes the layer "translucent," to let color layers show through.

8. Color

The color process for *Bandette* takes a little more explanation than we have room for here, and will be covered in part two. Long story short, I create new layers below the inks (Layer -> New -> Layer), which show through the ink layer. (*fig. 8*)

figure 8

9. Back up the inks

With the Magic Wand tool, I select the darkest areas of the ink layer. I create a new layer to go *between* the ink layer and the color layers. I fill the selection with a brown color. This assures that the color layer will not bleed through the art which is meant to read as "black." (*fig. 9*)

figure 9

10. Done!

Make all the layers visible by clicking on the little eye icon in the layers window. There you have it! It's a comic! (*fig. 10*)

figure 10

PART TWO: COLOR!

Before you start

Get ready! As seen in part one, I do all the lettering for the page before coloring the art, and then hide the lettering layers before moving on to colorize the inks, and change the blending mode of the ink layer to Multiply. Remember that all the coloring work will be on the color layers, but the ink layer will be visible so you can see what you're doing.

Why do I letter the art before I color it? Because if I find that I need to nudge the art or resize it a bit for word balloons, I can. Once the coloring is done, those adjustments are going to be a lot more difficult to make.

1. Prepare the first color layer

I use the Magic Wand tool to select the panel areas from the panel borders layer, create a new layer below the ink layer, and fill those selected pixels with a bright blue (or some other color that I know will contrast with the colors I will be using. This gives me selectable areas to work on as I color. (*fig. 1–2*)

figure 1

figure 2

2. Select and fill the main figures

On this first color layer, I fill the *main figures only* with a single color, using a combination of the Lasso tools, the Paintbucket tool, and the pencil setting of the Brush tool to select the areas. Whichever tools you use, be sure to have Anti-Aliasing checked *off*, and all opacity settings at 100%. The idea is to have hard edges between all shapes so you can select their pixels later. (*fig. 3–4*)

figure 3

figure 4

Why do I only fill in the main figures? Because I am going to color the background on a different layer. More on that later!

3. Color the main figures

Now that the areas of the main figures have been defined, I go back into those areas with the Lasso, Paintbucket, and/or the Brush tool, and color the individual parts. (*fig. 5–6*) I find that it is much quicker to select large areas to color and work my way down to the small detailed areas than it is to go the other way around.

figure 5

figure 6

4. Create a new layer for the background

Now I use the Magic Wand tool to select all the blue pixels that make up the background, create a new layer *above* the color layer I've been working on, and fill those pixels *only* with the yellow I use as a base color for all my backgrounds. It's kind of like putting down a primer coat before painting a wall. (*fig. 7–8*)

figure 7

figure 8

5. Color the background

I color details into those yellow background pixels, using the Lasso, Paintbucket, and Brush tools again. Again, it's more efficient to pick out the larger shapes (sky, house, ground, trees) and then go in and add details with the brush tool. That's most evident here on the house around the windows, and the bricks on the wall. (fig. 9–10)

figure 9

figure 10

You may have noticed that the background is done with a very limited number of colors. In fact, I try to only use values of *three hues* (yellow, green, and blue), which I have saved as preset color swatches. I very rarely deviate from these colors for backgrounds in daytime scenes. (fig. 11)

figure 11

Why such a limited color palette? Two reasons. First, it assures a pleasing continuity throughout the comic—nothing is going to hit you in the eyeball because it clashes with the rest of the world, unless I want it to. Second, it helps keep me from dithering over choices. Without this structure in place, I might very well spend a lot of wasted time trying to decide what colors to use. This way those choices have already been made, and I can just work.

7. Desaturate the background color layer

Almost done! But there's one more tweak to be made. This is why I do background colors on a separate layer! The colors I used for the background are paler than those I use for the main figures, but they're just as saturated, or intense, so they compete a bit for the eye's attention. By desaturating those colors a bit, the main figures pop out more!

Here's how: with the background layer selected, I go to Image –> Adjustments –> Hue/Saturation and set the saturation level at -40.

Now the final art (with the letters visible again) has a nice watercolor wash look to it! (*fig. 12*)

figure 12

Why do I not just use desaturated colors for the backgrounds to begin with? I could do that, but it's likely that I would forget which colors were the desaturated ones and which were not. It's much easier to color everything with the same color palette (I sometimes use background colors on figures as well) and adjust the saturation all at once.

And that is how I color *Bandette*!

SPECIAL THANKS

Paul

Special thanks to Chris Roberson and Allison Baker of Monkeybrain Comics, without whom Bandette would not exist. Thanks to Colleen, and to Nancy Drew, and Modesty Blaise, and thanks to every girl who has ever solved a mystery, or was brazen enough to dance along a rooftop.

Colleen

Thank you to Chris Roberson and Allison Baker for asking us to "come up with something" for their Monkeybrain Comics digital publishing experiment. Thank you to all our homies at Periscope Studio for being the best friends, colleagues, bros, and lady-bros anyone could wish for. Thanks to the 1960s, France, girl detectives, and cat burglars for continuously feeding our inspiration. Thanks to Dark Horse Comics for making *Bandette* a thing to hold in one's hands. Thank you to Paul for everything.

about the authors

Paul Tobin is the critically acclaimed writer of many, many things, including hundreds of comics for Marvel, DC, Dark Horse, and a nifty bunch of others, on such projects as his Dark Horse horror series *Colder* and *Gingerbread Girl* for Top Shelf. Paul is expanding his writing into prose with his debut novel *Prepare to Die!*, and he helps produce *Angry Birds* animation for the fine folks at Rovio. Paul enjoys burlesque shows, shopping for vintage clothing, soccer, and teenage detectives, and the list of characters he would enjoy writing includes Sherlock Holmes, Betty & Veronica, Nancy Drew, Uncle Scrooge, Corto Maltese, Charlie Brown, Modesty Blaise, and James Bond.

Colleen Coover is an illustrator and comic book artist/writer living in Portland, Oregon. She is the creator of the adult comic *Small Favors*, and artist of the all-ages *Banana Sunday* and the graphic novel *Gingerbread Girl*, both written by her husband Paul Tobin. She has worked for Marvel Comics, DC Comics, Dark Horse, Top Shelf Productions, Oni Press, Fantagraphics and many others. She spends most of her time thinking up way for comics to be more awesome.

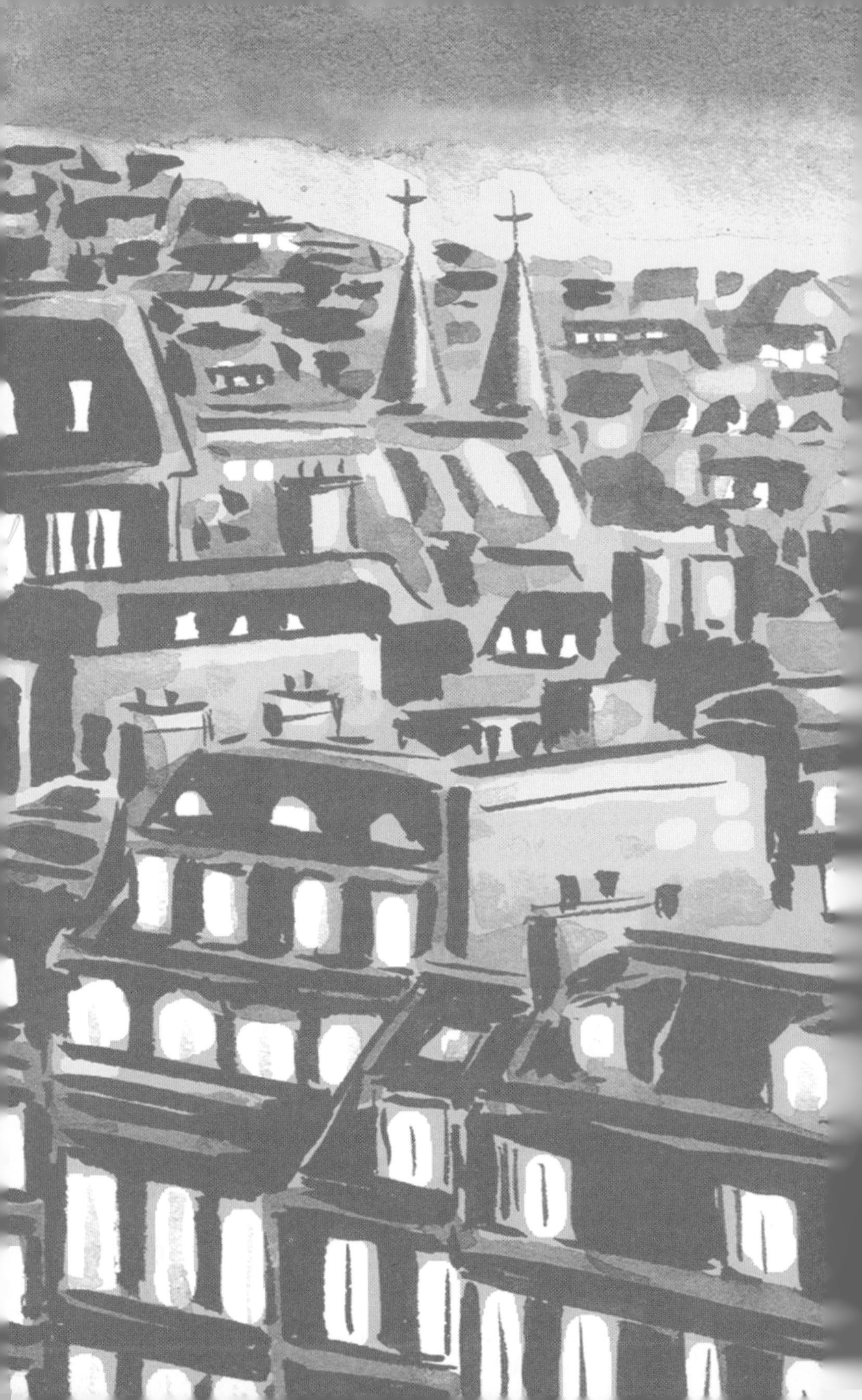